CHILDREN AS TEACHERS OF PEACE

love

me...

Susan C.

CHILDREN AS TEACHERS OF PEACE

By Our Children

Edited by **Gerald G. Jampolsky,** M.D., author of *Love is Letting Go of Fear*
with Cheryl Boyce, age 15, Eric Cutter, age 15, Krissy Drew, age 14, Mark Green, age 15, Tom Green, and Carol Howe.

Foreword by Hugh Prather

Celestial Arts Millbrae, California

Published by Celestial Arts, 231 Adrian Road, Millbrae, California 94030
Front cover drawing by Gregory Howe, age 11
Back cover drawing by Natashya Wilson, age 11
Title page drawing by Billy Adams, age 11

Proceeds from the sale of this book will go to the Foundation to further peace in the world.

First Printing, June 1982
Manufactured in the United States of America

1 2 3 4 5 6 7 8 88 87 86 85 84 83 82

Thank You

We wish to thank all the children, their parents and their teachers who have cooperated in this venture. It was very difficult to restrict ourselves to the examples included as there were so many wonderful entries from which to choose.

We are also very grateful to Dr. William Thetford, Patricia Hopkins, and Patty-Lynn Green for assisting with the selection and editing process; to David Suddendorf for his counsel; and to Aeesha Ababio, Dee Alarcon, Ron and Margaret Danzig, Ann Dunker, Gayle Prather, Gigi Talcott and Sandi Kalinowski for collecting and assembling the letters, pictures and statements used in this book.

The Editors

Many people have talked and written about how children think. I have read that children's thoughts tend to revolve around their personal concerns; that most children have little insight into their powers; that only through a great many meaningful experiences can a child understand.... And then we see the results of an assignment such as this one, and I think of the old cliche, "Out of the mouths of babes...."

George Cocores. Principal, Korn School
Durham, Connecticut

Foreword by Hugh Prather

Peace is the willingness to forgive, to overlook, and to see beyond it all, the smile of God. Peace is the willingness to be comfortable, to relax, and to slowly sink past all cares but the love that is of God. Love your brothers and sisters and all living things.

Peace is the willingness not to wait to see your way through, but to do it now, this instant. And what is there to do? Only this: Simply be at peace.

Children As Teachers of Peace

This book by our children is the result of a joyous journey. From the day we were inspired by the realization of the truth in the words "Children as Teachers of Peace"... to the invitation we issued that same week to children throughout the country to express their thoughts and advice about peace...to the day only five weeks later when this book was delivered to the publisher, we have been profoundly moved by the truth our children speak for all of us.

The Editors

Dedication

This book is dedicated to the many people all around the world to help make peace a reality.

Interduction

Open this book and let the sun shine in. Open this book and let your thoughts pour out. Open this book and let your understanding grow more. Open this book and let love flow!

This book was written for adults by kids! Because the simplest thoughts are somtimes the best. For peace is the goal of everyone not just you and me.

Lance Lawson
age 11

Peace Is. . . .
Save me, Please!
working together to keep every thing alive.
Blackfooted Ferret
John, age 11½

Suzanne, age 10

Peace is...

Peace is love between people. *Jessica, age 10*

Peace is when you have a soul. When you have a friend inside to be grateful fore. *Susanna, age 10*

Peace is a boy giving a girl a flower. *Lashawn, age 6*

Peace is when you share a piece of gum with your friend. *Paxton, age 10*

Peace is two nations shaking hands and being friends forever. *Lauren, age 12*

Peace is having time to sit by yourself and not to have to think in the past about what is going to happen to you. *Adam, age 12*

Pease is friends who get along and make up when they fight. *Sari, age 10*

Peace is not fighting because the world may die. Peace begins with me and my mom and dad. How can we teach peace to the world? *Alisa, age 8*

Peace is a friendship dance that everyone holds hands in. *Dana, age 9*

Peace is being quiet so the pastor can talk. *Nathan, age 5*

Peace is fun! *Brian, age 7*

Peace is telling the truth to your parents or anybody. *Jeremy, age 8*

Peace is happiness when it rains and we see a rainbow. *Arthur, age 6*

Peace is birds because they hardly ever fight. *Allan, age 10*

Tappié, age 11

Peace

Peace is caring for those around you.
Peace is all Nations joining hands
Peace is not desroying gods creation
Peace is knowing the meaning of Love
Peace will only happen if everyone works together.

Sirena, age 10

Peace

Peace is caring for those around you.
Peace is all Nations joining hands
Peace is not desroying gods creation
Peace is knowing the meaning of Love
Peace will only happen if everyone works toghether.

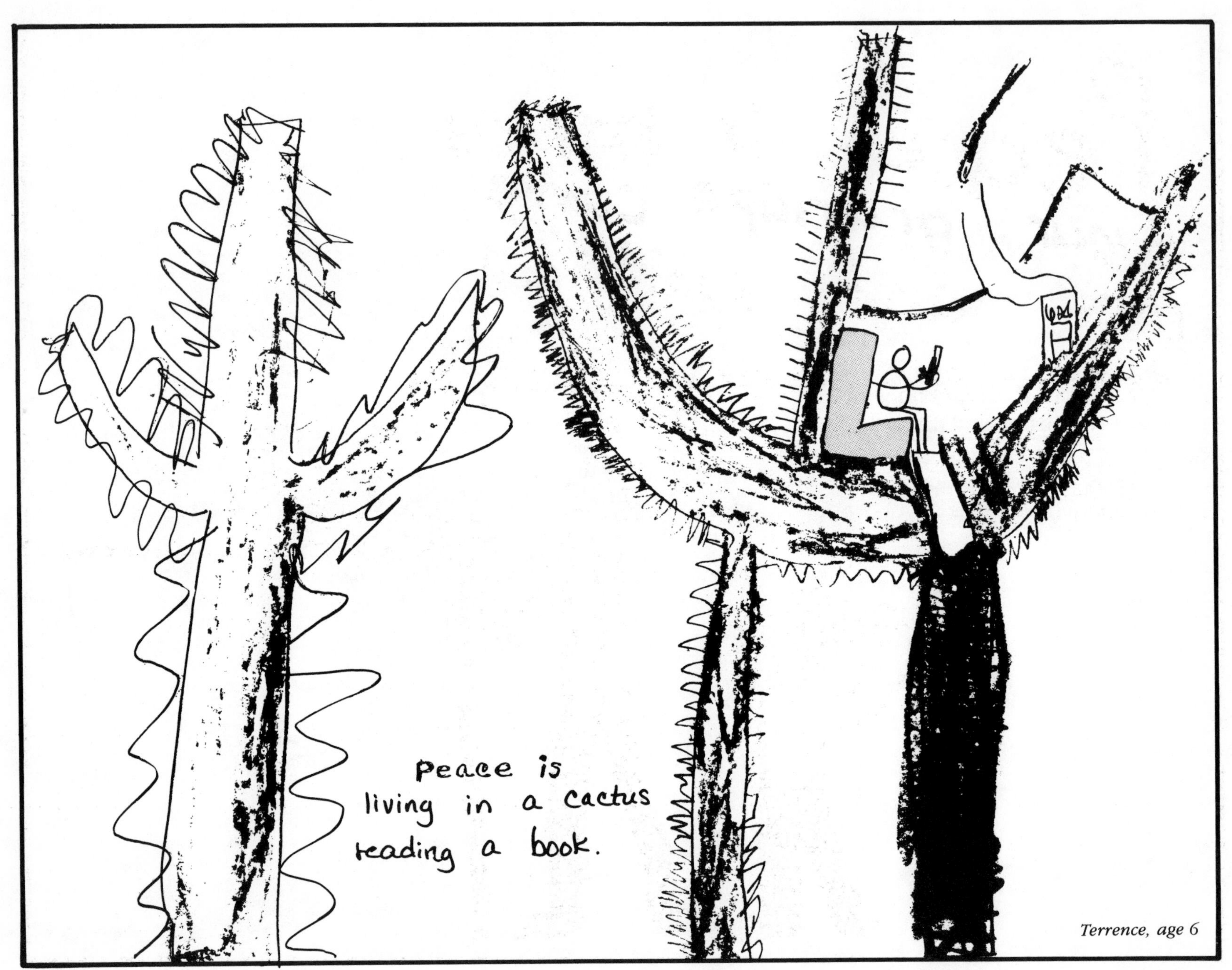

Terrence, age 6

Peace is having your grandpa come over and spoil you for a couple of days.

Chuck, age 9

Tom [illegible]
12

Peace is ——

Peace is to stop fighting after many days, weeks, months, or years. To stop shooting people and blowing up buildings and cars and trucks and every thing else in sight. Peace is making an agreement after arguing for hours of who gets to use the car tonite. Peace is to stop beeting up your sister because she stole your superman toilet paper and she turned off your favarite show that you have been waiting to watch all week and so happy when it comes time to watch it and your sister turns it of.

Peace is...

Peace is to stop fighting after many days, weeks, months, or years. To stop shooting people and blowing up buildings and cars and trucks and everything else in sight. Peace is making an agreement after arguing for hours of who gets to use the car tonite. Peace is to stop beeting up your sister because she stole your superman toilet paper and she turned off your favorite show that you have been waiting to watch all week and so happy when it comes time to watch it and your sister turns it of.

Tom, age 12

Leigh, age 11

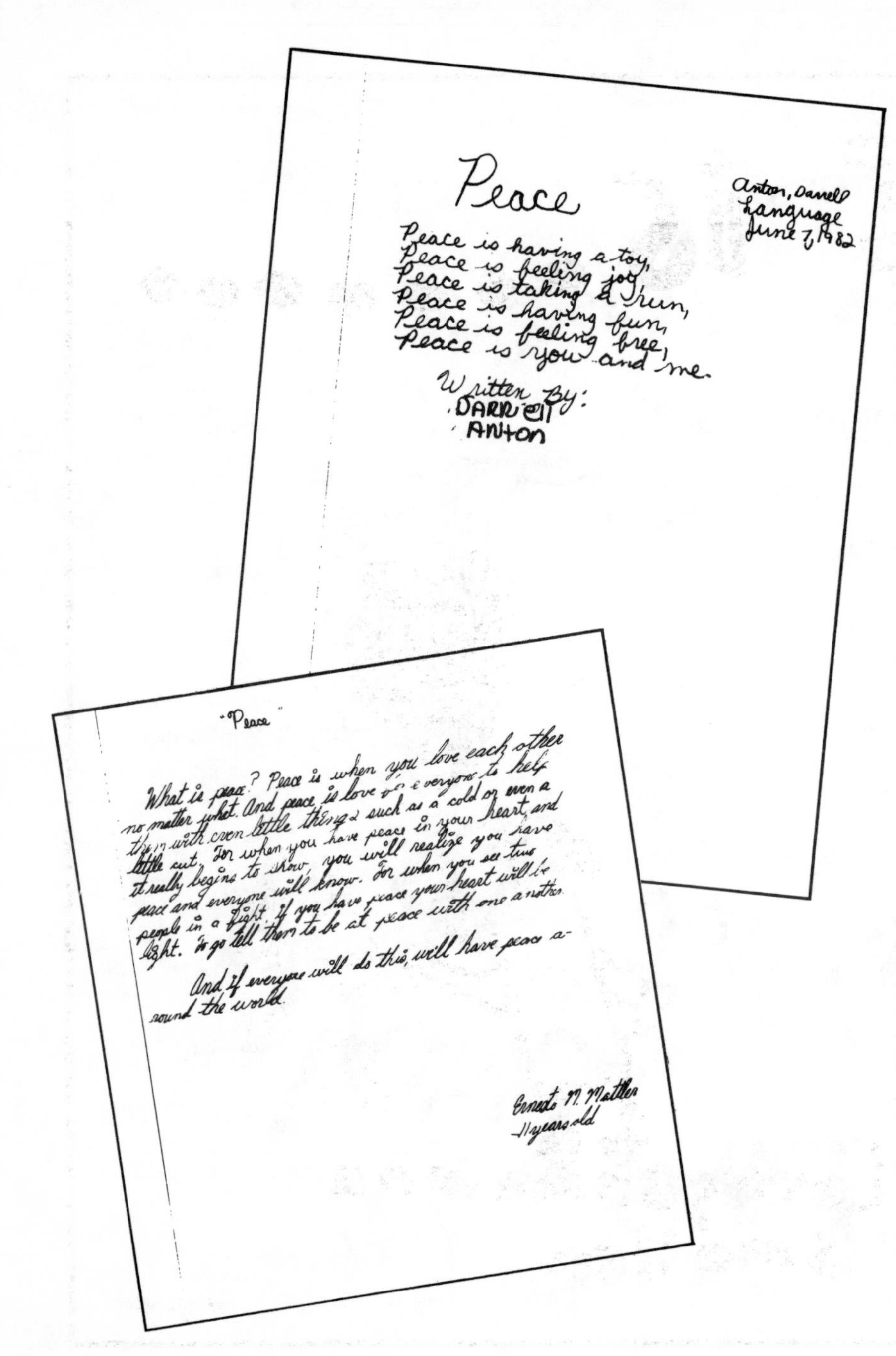
Peace

Anton, Darrell
Language
June 7, 1982

Peace is having a toy,
Peace is feeling joy,
Peace is taking a run,
Peace is having fun,
Peace is feeling free,
Peace is you and me.

Written By:
DARRELL
ANTON

"Peace"

What is peace? Peace is when you love each other no matter what. And peace is love for everyone to help them with even little things such as a cold or even a little cut. For when you have peace in your heart, and it really begins to show, you will realize you have peace and everyone will know. For when you see two people in a fight, if you have peace your heart will be light. To go tell them to be at peace with one another.

And if everyone will do this, will have peace around the world.

Ernesto M. Mattler
11 years old

Peace

Peace is having a toy,
Peace is feeling joy,
Peace is taking a run,
Peace is having fun,
Peace is feeling free,
Peace is you and me.

Darrell, age 12

"Peace"

What is peace? Peace is when you love each other no matter what. And peace is love for everyone to help them with even little things such as a cold or even a little cut. For when you have peace in your heart, and it really begins to show, you will realize you have peace and everyone will know. For when you see two people in a fight, if you have peace your heart will be light. To go tell them to be at peace with one another.

And if everyone will do this, we'll have peace around the world.

Ernesto, age 11

PEACE is.......

Loving Someone

Loving someone smaller.

Carey, age 9

Peace by Haley mitchell age 8
peace is the sun that gives us
light and keeps us warm. Peace
is the moon glows and shows and
keeps us out of fright, In the night,
peace is every little thing that grows
and shows how much it cares.
It's the meadows soft green grass;
the animals out of danger; waterfalls
flowing and you knowing that the
world is safe. NO war! NO killing the
animals or anything, a bed of daisies
100 miles each way; a sweet smell in
the air; butterflies and buttercups
of of wondros colors; trees spreading
seeds all over the ground and all
you hear is the trees blowing; the wings
of the butterfly. of course this is only
my idea why don't you write yours?

Haley mitchell age 8

Peace

Peace is the sun that gives us light and keeps us warm. Peace is the moon glows and shows and keeps us out of fright. In the night, peace is every little thing that grows and shows how much it cares. It's the meadows soft green grass; the animals out of danger; waterfalls flowing and you knowing that the world is safe. NO war! NO killing the animals or anything, a bed of daisies 100 miles each way; a sweet smell in the air; butterflies and buttercups of wondros colors; trees spreading seeds all over the ground and all you hear is the trees blowing; the wings of the butterfly. Of course this is only my idea why don't you write yours?

Haley, age 8

Haley, age 8

Peace is. . . .

Peace is something you don't see much of anymore.

To me, peace is something to honor or else you might lose it. The things that go with peace are *very* important too. Things like trust, respect, love, and honor. These things are a necessity if you want to get, or keep peace.

In my opinion most people want peace, but aren't sure how to get it. And most of our treaties aren't doing much. In the Falkland's we signed a treaty saying we'll give arms to certain countries (among them Argentina and Britain). When two of those countries go to war, we are in trouble. No matter what our choice is, we get an eternal enemy.

Peace is something to cherish. But you must be careful with it. If you don't pretty soon there won't be anyone to make peace with.

The
End

Lori, age 11

PEACE IS...
A SCARCE THING
LORI Divita : 11

peace is being quiet alone in a very
small bedroom that is messy.
Peace is also being alone
petting my bunny rabbits in
the shade. Peace is waiting
for my mom to get
home from work.

Peace is being quiet alone in a very small bedroom that is messy.
Peace is also being alone petting my bunny rabbits in the shade.
Peace is waiting for my mom to get home from work.

Adam, age 10

Peace Is...
When people get along
And it doesn't take
so long.
When black and white
make friends.
So people don't need to
defend.
Not when countrys fight,
For justice and their own
rights.
That drugs can be
controlled.
When people aren't left
cold.
When people can have
food
When people aren't so
rude.
And when people read
all of the above,
So there can be
peace and love.
Holy Spirit Leigh Whelan
age-12
grade-6

Peace Is...

When people get along
And it doesn't take so long.
When black and white make friends
So people don't need to defend.
Not when countries fight
For justice and their own rights.
That drugs can be controlled.
When people aren't left cold.
When people can have food.
When people aren't so rude.
And when people read all of the above
So there can be peace and love.

Leigh, age 12

Peace is lying down under a pine tree with my rabbit licking my hands clean.
Diane Rummel
Age 11

Christine Hwang Age 6
Peace is a birthday party.

PEACE
IS
NATURAL
Terri, 8 ½

Peace Is...

Peace is people talking together with a heart in between them. *Siri Guru Dev Kaur, age 5*

Peace is people having fun in caves.
Ek Ong Kar Singh, age 6

Peace is having a friend. *Shae, age 10*

Peace is praying. *Siobhain, age 6*

Peace is seeing a baby learn to walk or to do something which they have never done before. Peace is being able to live and laugh and love without threats of nuclear wars or World War III. *Kendra, age 11*

Peace is people who shake hands and stuff like that.
Michael, age 9

Peace is fun but sometimes its boring. *Allison, age 9*

Peace is:
A quiet countryside with birds chirping and *no* arguments.
A snowy white day with deers hunting for food and *no* hunters.
A big green forest with rabbits running around and *no* forest fire.
The world we live in *if* we took care of it better.
Shannon, age 11

Peace is sitting near the fire with a warm cat snuggled in your lap purring. *Jennifer, age 9*

Peace is a lion and a lamb walking together! *Joan, age 9*

Peace is a soft rabbit. *Heather, age 11*

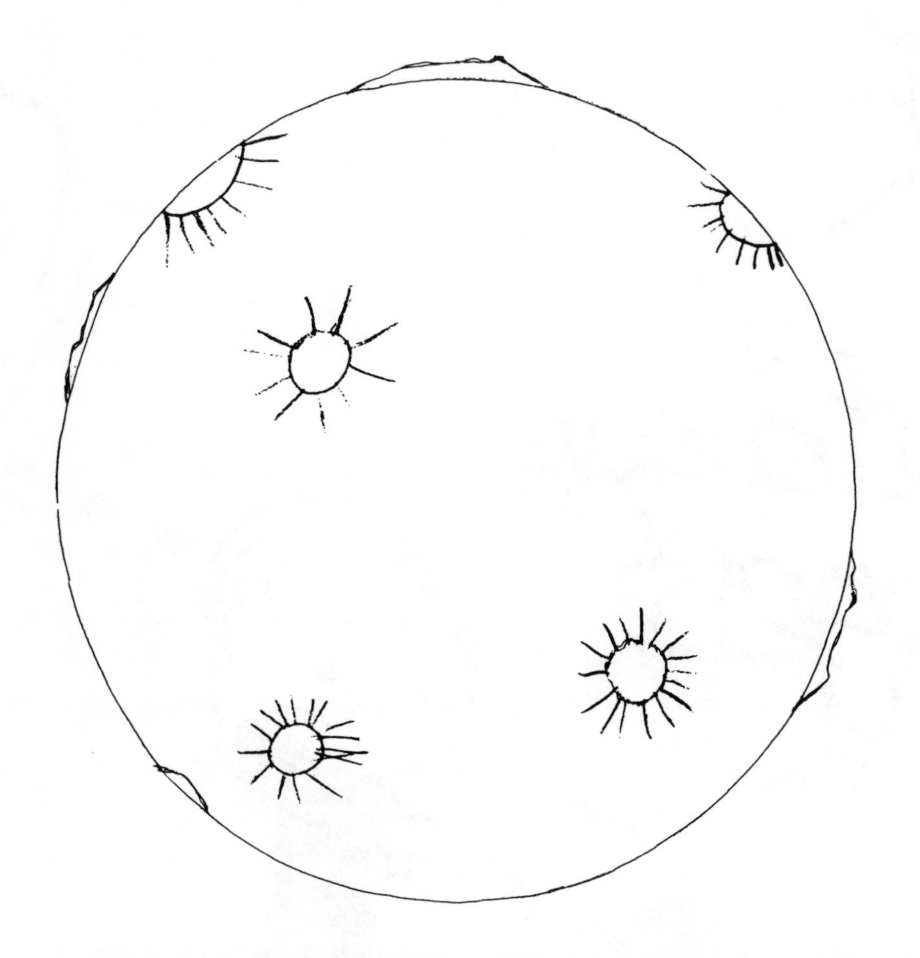

Peter, age 12

Peace
NaMe Stacy
Age 6
God

Peace

Peace is something big.
Peace is in our hearts.
It's in our minds we sing.
It's something that has no parts.
Live in peace,
or friendship at least.
Peace; make something of it, please!

Kariena, age 9

Peace is...

I think peace is having God holding
your hand every step you take.
Peace begins...
Peace begins with Love from God!

Charlene, age 12

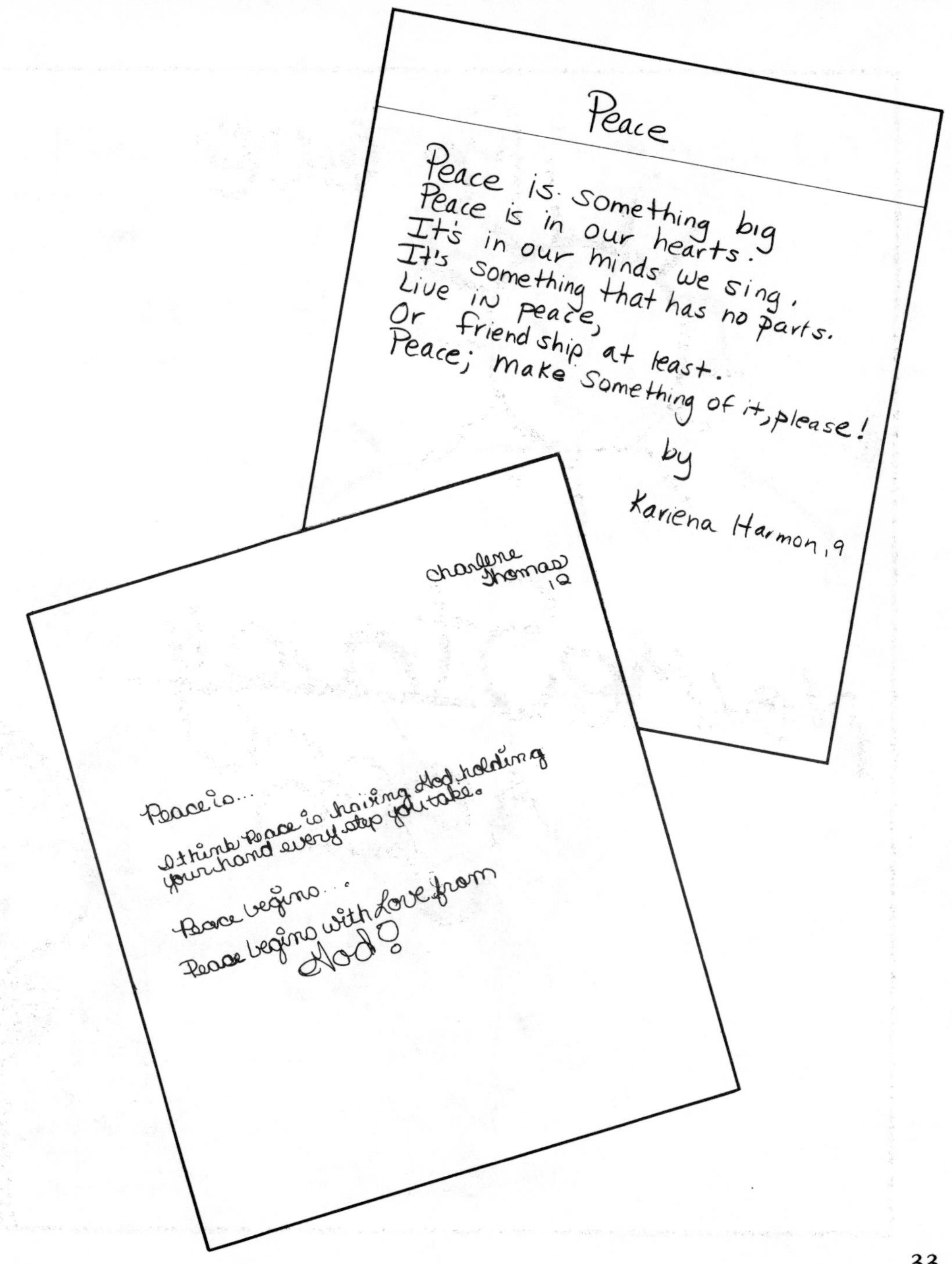

Peace

Peace is something big
Peace is in our hearts.
It's in our minds we sing,
It's something that has no parts.
Live in peace,
Or friendship at least.
Peace; make Something of it, please!

by

Kariena Harmon, 9

Charlene Thomas
12

Peace is...

I think Peace is having God holding
your hand every step you take.

Peace begins...

Peace begins with Love from
God!

PEACE IS THE WHOLE UNIVERSE WITHOUT FIGHTING:
LET'S NOT FIGHT
US NEITHER
Martion Mobile
CRISTA HARGREAVES 10¾

Peace is every one following the golden rule

Christine Joy
age10

Christine, age 10

Peace is friendship with someone.

Jenni Simpson
age 10

Peace is a feeling of love, of belonging. It is a feeling you feel when someone says something kind to you. It is something that all countries plead for, but, as is obvious, is hard to get. Peace can only be gotten when someone is kind or helpful to someone else. Peace is a sense of love, kindness and friendliness.

Peace is when there is no unhappiness, when there is no war, or loneliness. Peace is what an old man feels when someone helps him across the street. Peace is what a dog that was lost feels, when it finds its home. Peace is when someone is totally happy, warm, and wanted by other people.

Peace is achieved when two people, countries or animals make friends and are kind to each other. Peace is two friends, two happy, caring people.

Katy, age 12

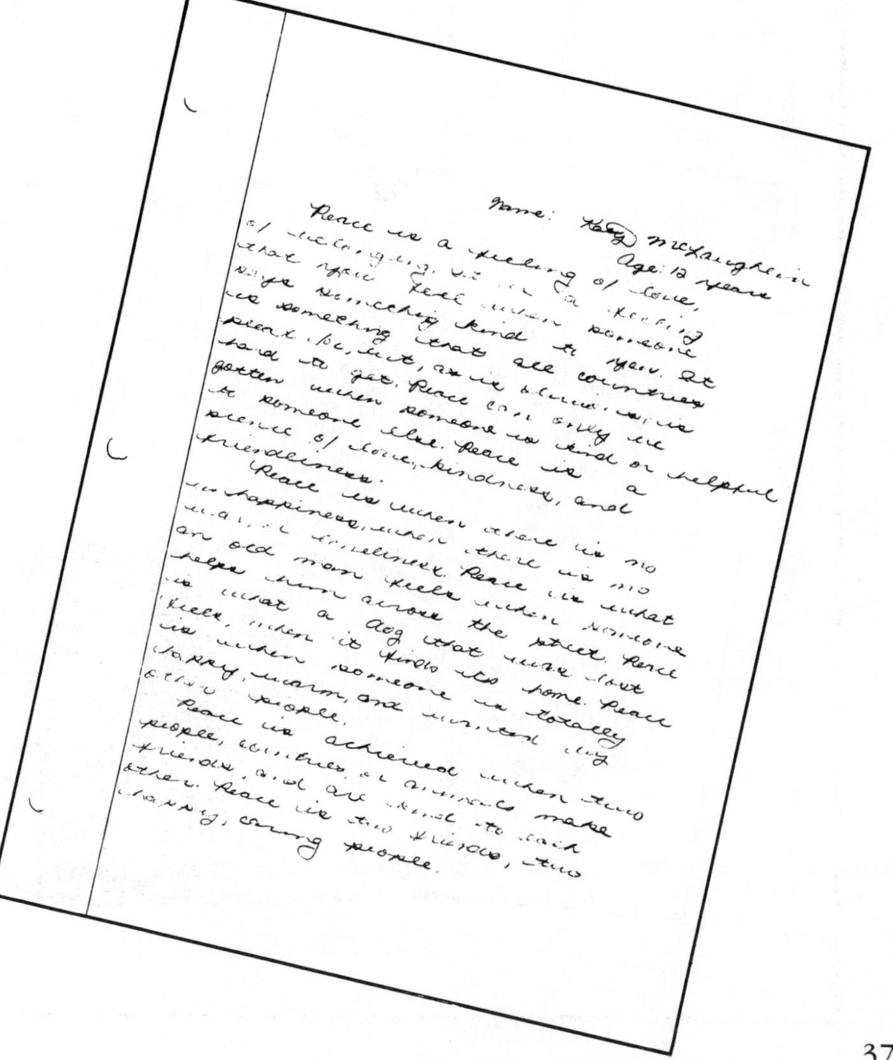

Name: Katy McLaughlin
Age: 12 years

Peace is a feeling of love, of belonging. It is a feeling that you feel when someone says something kind to you. It is something that all countries plead for, but, as is obvious, is hard to get. Peace can only be gotten when someone is kind or helpful to someone else. Peace is a sense of love, kindness, and friendliness.

Peace is when there is no unhappiness, when there is no war, or loneliness. Peace is what an old man feels when someone helps him across the street. Peace is what a dog that was lost feels, when it finds its home. Peace is when someone is totally happy, warm, and wanted by other people.

Peace is achieved when two people, countries, or animals make friends, and are kind to each other. Peace is two friends, two happy, caring people.

Peace to me is:

That apple that is high on a branch on your tree—it's just out of your reach. Yet if we want it bad enough we will make that extra effort to go in the garage and get a ladder!

I feel peace is just like that apple. It's just out of reach, but if we make that extra effort we can have the apple, the peace!

If all the generals, sargents, presidents & leaders would just focus on one thing "love."

Love & Peace go together like pen & paper, like teeth & gums, like a grapes & a vine!

Love & Peace are two things everyone can have even you!

Lance, age 11

PEACE
is riding
in the
Forest
Kathy
mcDonald
age 12

Matt, age 6

Peace Is...

Peace is catching bubbles. *Ryan, age 6½*

Peace is planting flowers on a clear day.
Michelle, age 10

Peace is when I'm alone at home when its raining.
Cassie, age 7

Peace is the trees And the gentle breeze
The buzzing bees And the little fleas. *Penny, age 11*

Peace is sleeping with your dog. *Michael, age 7*

Peace is having a picnic under the moon.
Yolanda, age 10

Peace is when somebody reaches out to somebody else.
Kerri, age 10

Peace means you don't go around the street robbing and stealing stores. Sometimes life is like a nightmare.
John, age 10

Peace is when you're laying in your bed and thinking about some things. *Michelle, age 6*

Peace is 4 little kittens sleeping with there mother, and no one to bother them. *Sandy, age 10*

Peace is made by friendship, love and people.
Heather, age 11

Peace is sleeping in the car. *Justin, age 7*

Peace should be one big, happy world. *John, age 10*

Pees mees cwit. [Peace means quiet.] *Bethany, age 7*

Peace is sitting in a field of wild iris flowers. Peace is having fun. Peace is sitting with baby, fuzzy kittens.
Melissa, age 10

Peace is when kids are taking naps. And parents are alone downstairs drinking wine and talking.
Larisa, age 9

Peace is trees, not stumps. *James, age 7*

What peace means to me is Presidents, chancellors and leaders sitting in the U.N. and talking and laughing.
Jeff, age 12

Brett, age 13

(Drawing submitted unsigned.)

Peace is when the wind stops blowing. Peace is when the sun is showing. Know that my Daddy's home. God gives me Peace, Peace, Peace. I think I understand, Peace, Peace is holding Jesus' hand. Peace is when everyone is happy and laughing. Peace is when nobody is fighting. Peace is when the trees are rocking back and forth. Peace is when you are home alone drawing a picture. Peace is when you are reading the Bible alone. Peace is when your mommy or Daddy is huging you. Peace is when no body is yelling and shouting. Peace is when you watch the T.V. alone

Marilee, age 8

Marla, age 10

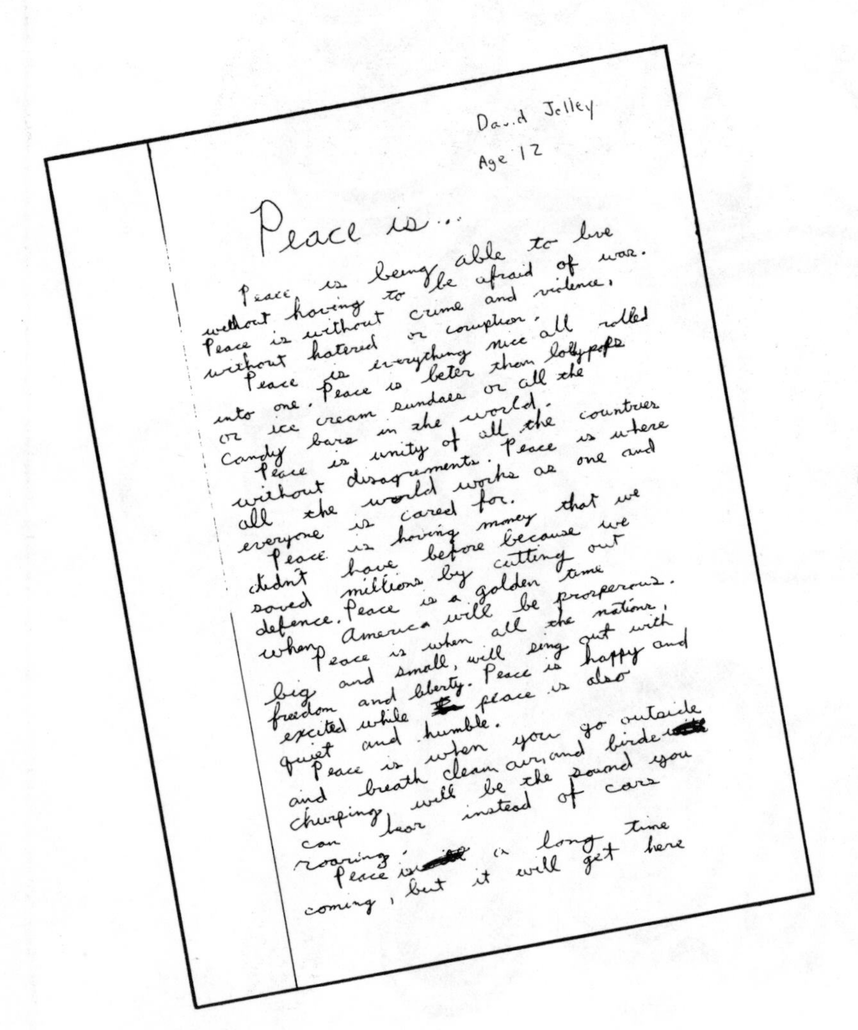

David Jelley
Age 12

Peace is...

Peace is being able to live
without having to be afraid of war.
Peace is without crime and violence,
without hatered or coruption.
Peace is everything nice all rolled
into one. Peace is beter than lolypops
or ice cream sundaes or all the
candy bars in the world.
Peace is unity of all the countries
without disagrements. Peace is where
all the world works as one and
everyone is cared for.
Peace is having money that we
didnt have before because we
saved millions by cutting out
defence. Peace is a golden time
when America will be prosperous.
Peace is when all the nations,
big and small, will sing out with
freedom and liberty. Peace is happy and
excited while peace is also
quiet and humble.
Peace is when you go outside
and breath clean air, and birds
chirping will be the sound you
can hear instead of cars
roaring.
Peace is a long time
coming, but it will get here

Peace is. . . .

Peace is being able to live without having to be afraid of war. Peace is without crime and violence, without hatered or coruption.

Peace is everything nice all rolled into one. Peace is beter than lolypops or ice cream sundaes or all the candy bars in the world.

Peace is unity of all the countries without disagreements. Peace is where all the world works as one and everyone is cared for.

Peace is having money that we didn't have before because we saved millions by cutting out defence. Peace is a golden time when America will be prosperous.

Peace is when all the nations, big and small, will sing out with freedom and liberty. Peace is happy and excited while peace is also quiet and humble.

Peace is when you go outside and breath clean air, and birds chirping will be the sound you can hear instead of cars roaring.

Peace is a long time coming, but it will get here

David, age 12

Robert, age 11

PEACE IS LOVE THAT IS
PASSED ON FROM GENERATION TO GENERATION.
CLIFFORD AGE 8½

Carrie Taylor
Age 6

Peace is
smelling a tree.

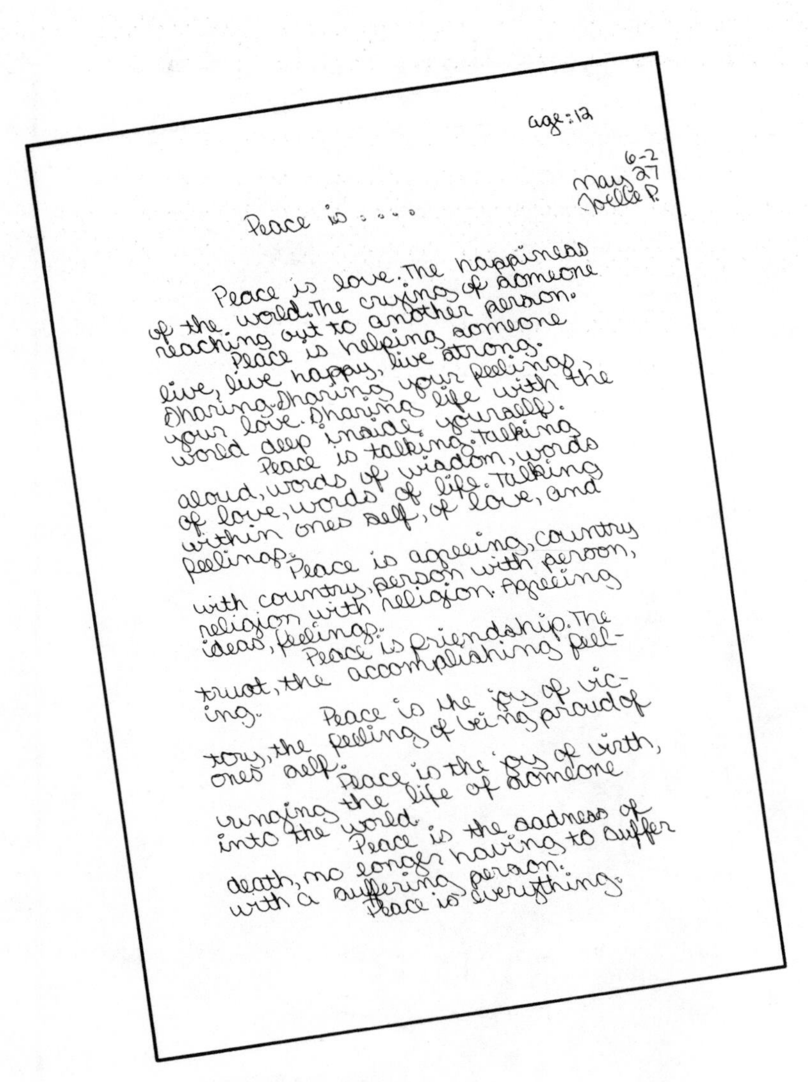

age: 12

6-2
May 27
Joelle P.

Peace is ....

Peace is love. The happiness of the world. The crying of someone reaching out to another person.

Peace is helping someone live, live happy, live strong. Sharing. Sharing your feelings, your love. Sharing life with the world deep inside yourself.

Peace is talking. Talking aloud, words of wisdom, words of love, words of life. Talking within ones self, of love, and feelings.

Peace is agreeing, country with country, person with person, religion with religion. Agreeing ideas, feelings.

Peace is friendship. The trust, the accomplishing feeling.

Peace is the joy of victory, the feeling of being proud of ones self.

Peace is the joy of birth, bringing the life of someone into the world.

Peace is the sadness of death, no longer having to suffer with a suffering person.

Peace is everything.

Peace is...

Peace is love. The happiness of the world. The crying of someone reaching out to another person.

Peace is helping someone live, live happy, live strong. Sharing. Sharing your feelings, your love. Sharing life with the world deep inside yourself.

Peace is talking. Talking aloud, words of wisdom, words of love, words of life. Talking within ones self, of love, of feelings.

Peace is agreeing, country with country, person with person, religion with religion. Agreeing ideas, feelings.

Peace is friendship. The trust, the accomplishing feeling.

Peace is the joy of victory, the feeling of being proud of ones self.

Peace is the joy of birth, bringing the life of someone into the world.

Peace is the sadness of death, no longer having to suffer with a suffering person.

Peace is everything.

Joelle, age 12

Peace in the Air

Peace is in the air everybody can have it nobody can steal it we all can share it in the world. Peace is a speical thought or a special love or light or spark that we all share within ourseleves. If there was peace there would be no wars or fights just a special love all over the world.

Joel, age 11

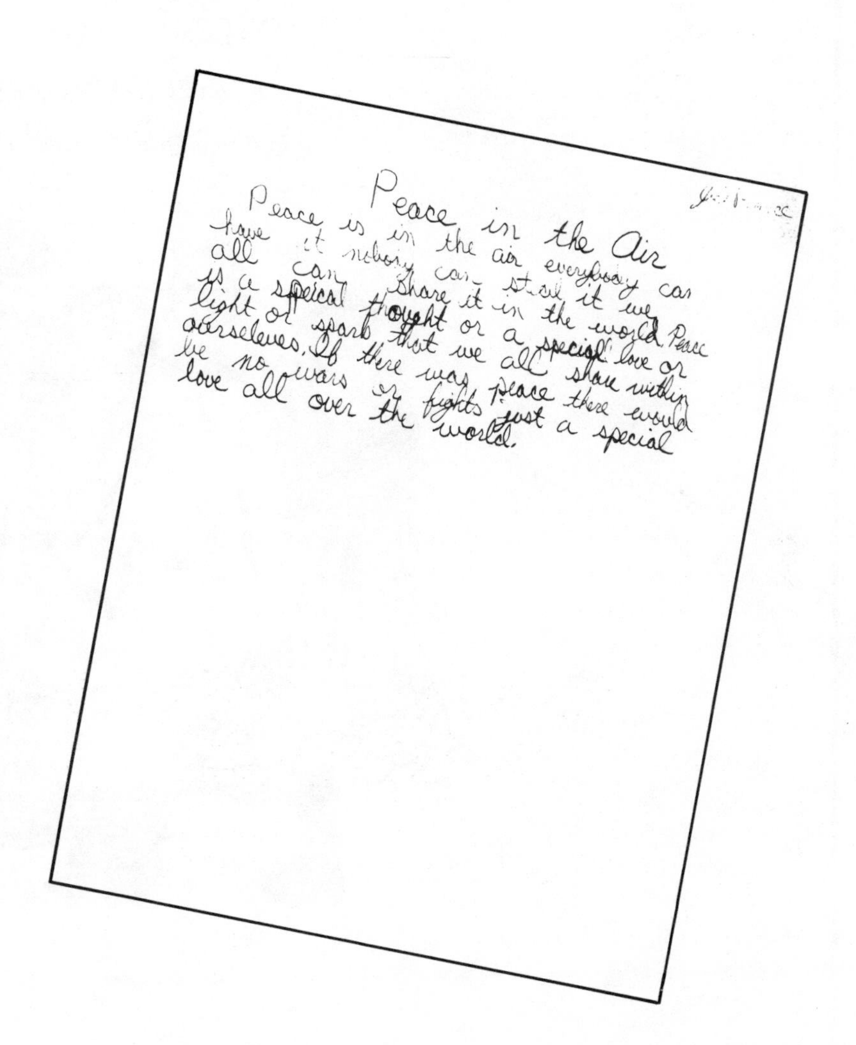

Peace in the Air

Peace is in the air everybody can
have it nobody can steal it we
all can share it in the world. Peace
is a speical thought or a special love or
light or spark that we all share within
ourseleves. If there was peace there would
be no wars or fights just a special
love all over the world.

Christine O'Keeffe
Age 12

Peace is when people do not fight. There is no prejudice. And all people join as one, each person their very best self.

Peace is...

Peas is God. *Marnie, age 5*

Peace means I love my mom. *Megan, age 5*

Peace means communicating. *Elizabeth, age 10*

Peace means sharing money and love with the poor. It will put a smile on their faces. *Linda, age 9*

Peace is a state of public calmness. *Amy, age 10*

Peace is being up sick all night with someone by your side. *Nancy, age 10*

Peace is like Angels, they are Love. *Jim, age 11*

Peace has no meaning any more. Ever since I was born, there has been some peace disturbance. Vietnam, Iran, Pakistan, etc. There should be something done.
Sonny, age 10

Peace is not stopping someone from believing what they want to. Like the easter bunny or Santa Claus.
Cooper, age 9

Peace is a time where everyone is satisfied with who and where they are. There is no grumbling about this or that. No one strives to change the world around him or her. Also, no one tries to get in a better position.
Sherief, age 11

Peace is no school, no homework, no teachers. Pizza, friends, designer clothing, boyfriends, a trip to New York and money. *Renee, age 10*

Peace is love! Love is the greatest peace I think we have and if it stops, we stop and start fighting. *Deanna, age 11*

Peace means to me to wait patiently for my mother to come to pik me up. *Julianne, age 7*

Peace is enemies loving one another, forever.
Trace, age 9

Peace is everything a person needs. It's stillness, faith, calmness and love all together and that's what I think peace is. *Jesse, age 11*

What's important is what peace means to you. What is your experience of peace?

Peace is. . . .

Written by ______________ Age______

Peace Is...

Drawn by______________________________ Age__________

Judith, age 11

What Peace Means to Me

Hello Hello
peace is a very good thing you know.
So show that you know
That peace can be spread
Throughout the world!
Hello Hello.

Mark, age 6

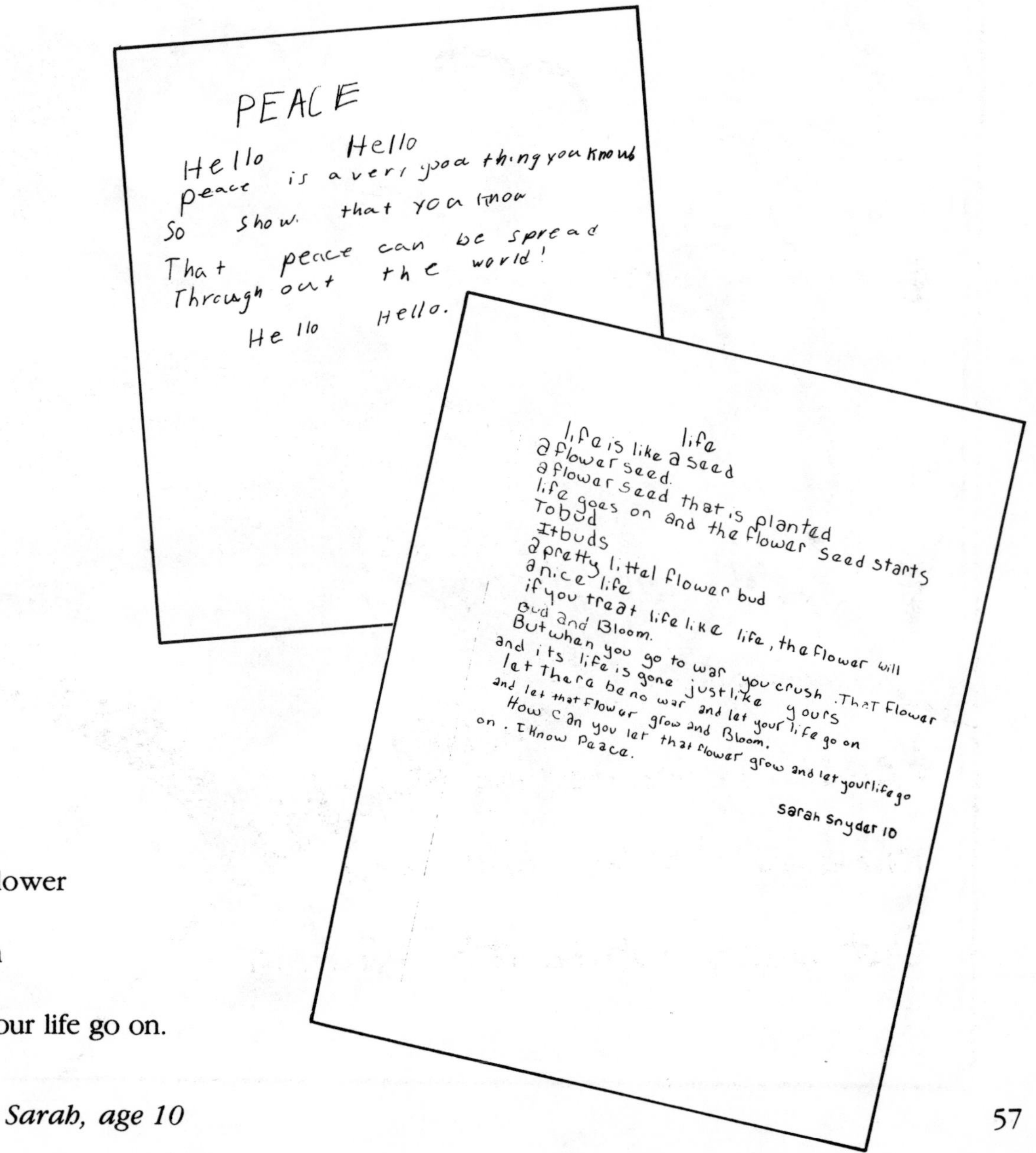

PEACE

Hello Hello
peace is a very good thing you know
So show that you know
That peace can be spread
Through out the world!
Hello Hello.

life

life is like a seed
a flower seed.
a flower seed that is planted
life goes on and the flower seed starts
To bud
It buds
a pretty littel flower bud
a nice life
if you treat life like life, the flower will
Bud and Bloom.
But when you go to war you crush That Flower
and its life is gone just like yours
let there be no war and let your life go on
and let that Flower grow and Bloom.
How can you let that flower grow and let your life go
on. I know Peace.

Sarah Snyder 10

Life

Life is like a seed
a flower seed.
a flower seed that is planted
life goes on and the flower seed starts
to bud
It buds
a pretty littel flower bud
a nice life
if you treat life like life, the Flower will
Bud and Bloom.
But when you go to war you crush that Flower
and its life is gone just like yours
let there be no war and let your life go on
and let that Flower grow and Bloom.
How can you let that flower grow and let your life go on.
I know Peace.

Sarah, age 10

Amana, age 10

THIS IS WHAT

PEACE MEANS

TO

ME

Peace

Peace

PEACE

Amynah, age 10½

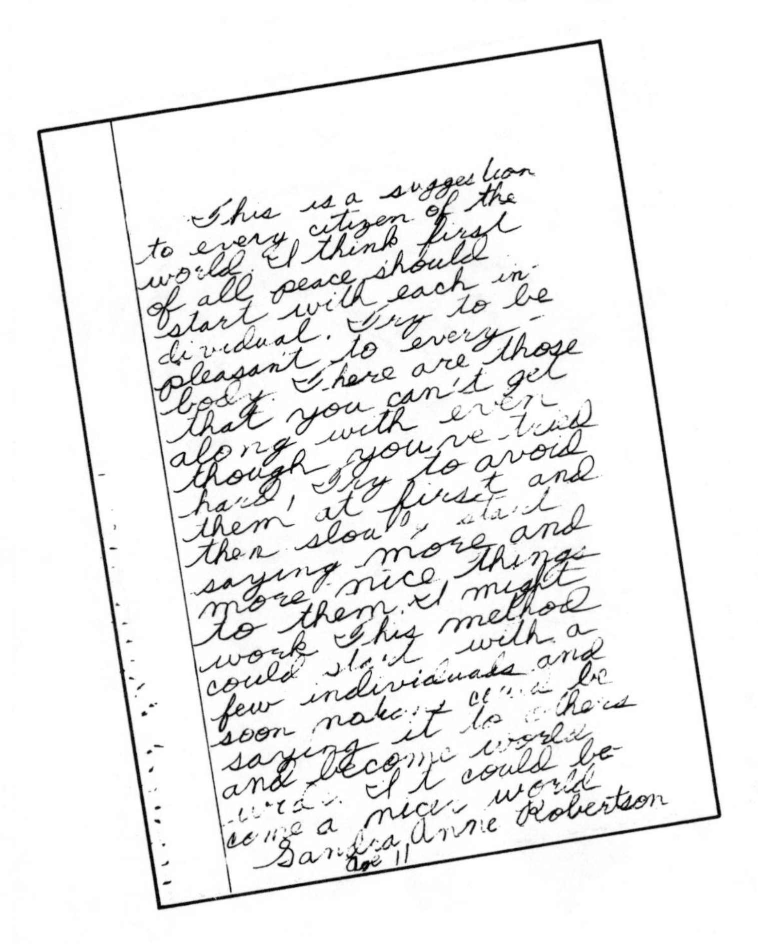

This is a suggestion
to every citizen of the
world. I think first
of all peace should
start with each in-
dividual. Try to be
pleasant to every-
body. There are those
that you can't get
along with even
though you've tried
hard. Try to avoid
them at first and
then slowly start
saying more and
more nice things
to them. It might
work. This method
could start with a
few individuals and
soon nations could be
saying it to others
and become world
wide. It could be-
come a nicer world
Sandra Anne Robertson
Age 11

What peace means to me....

This is a suggestion to every citizen of the world. I think first of all peace should start with each individual. Try to be pleasant to everybody. There are those that you can't get along with even though you've tried hard. Try to avoid them at first and then slowly start saying more and more nice things to them. It might work. This method could start with a few individuals and soon nations could be saying it to others and become world wide. It could become a nicer world.

Sandra Anne, age 11

Peace

Why can't we have peace in this world?

Is there a rule that says we can't have some peace in this world?

Why do some people have to argue?

If people would just realize that every person in this world is a human being. Just like us there's no difference at all. People have feelings and have a heart, also. We all need peace!! If there was nothing else but peace there wouldn't be any wars. We would know more about ourselves. If we didn't have wars we would be able to live without fear. But we're all humans, and humans make mistakes. When people argue and don't communicate and that how wars start!! If two contries are in an argument instead of starting a war they should talk it out!!

Wednesday, age 11

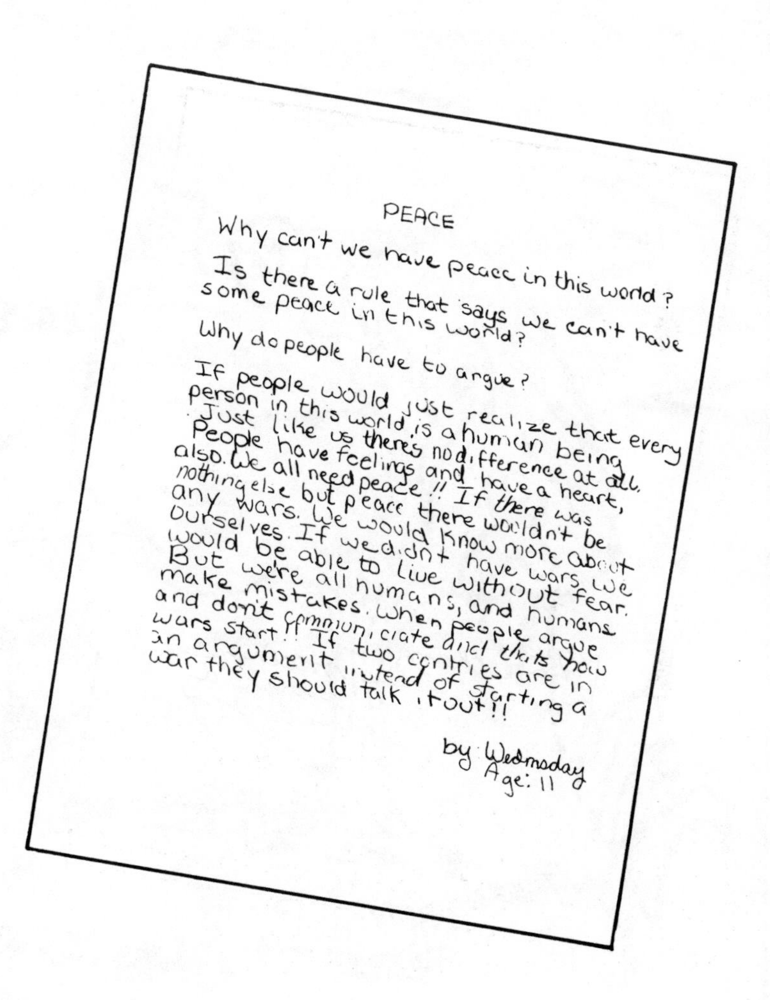
PEACE
Why can't we have peace in this world?
Is there a rule that says we can't have some peace in this world?
Why do people have to argue?
If people would just realize that every person in this world is a human being. Just like us there's no difference at all. People have feelings and have a heart, also. We all need peace!! If there was nothing else but peace there wouldn't be any wars. We would know more about ourselves. If we didn't have wars we would be able to live without fear. But we're all humans, and humans make mistakes. When people argue and don't communiciate and that's how wars start!! If two contries are in an argument intead of starting a war they should talk it out!!

by Wednsday
Age: 11

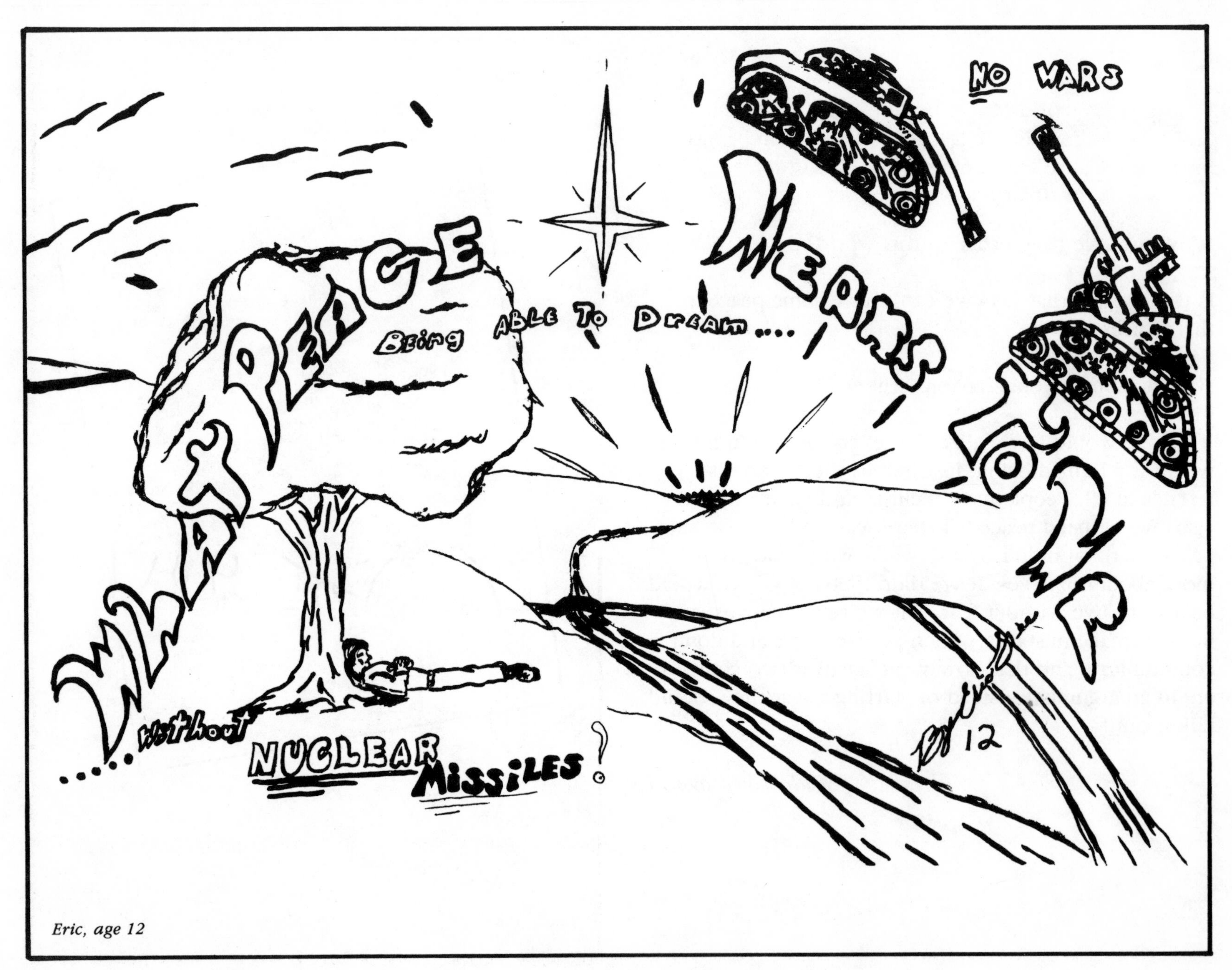
NO WARS
WHAT PEACE MEANS TO ME
Being ABLE To Dream....
....without NUCLEAR MISSILES?
12

Eric, age 12

We need world peace. If we don't have world peace we could ruin the last soarce of human beings anywhere. There are so many people that don't want to have war that I don't see why we even have to question it. If only we could get through peoples mind that we can live on what we have, we don't need everything in the world. This is the only world we know of, so let's not ruin it.

Marc, age 9

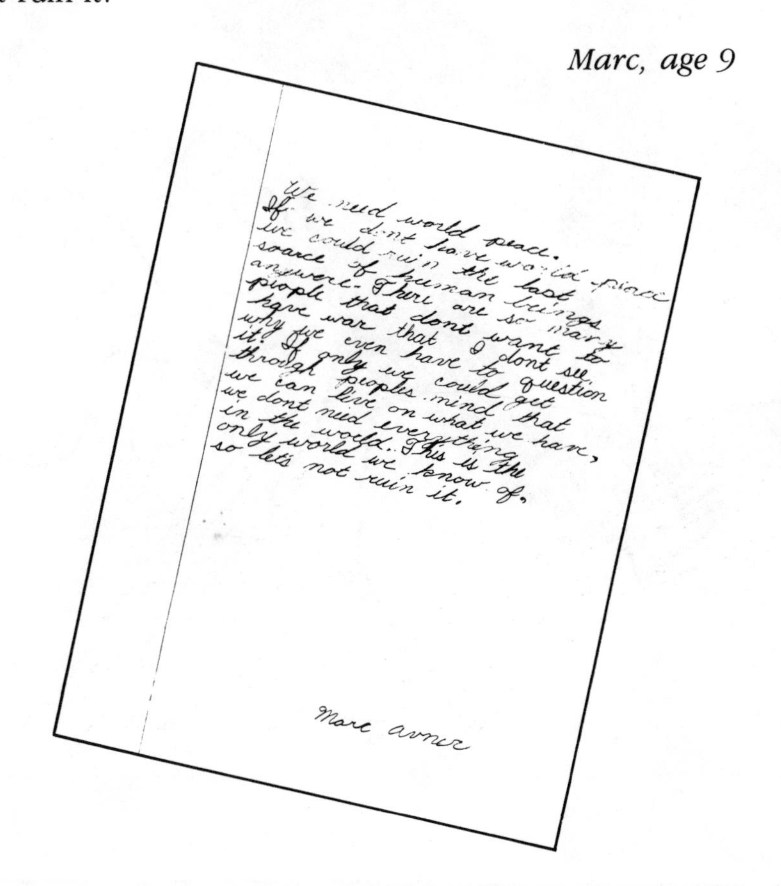

We need world peace.
If we dont have world peace
we could ruin the last
soarce of human beings
anywere. There are so many
people that dont want to
have war that I dont see
why we even have to question
it. If only we could get
through peoples mind that
we can live on what we have,
we dont need everything
in the world. This is the
only world we know of,
so let's not ruin it.

Marc avner

Gurumittar Singh, age 6

Gurumittar Singh, age 6

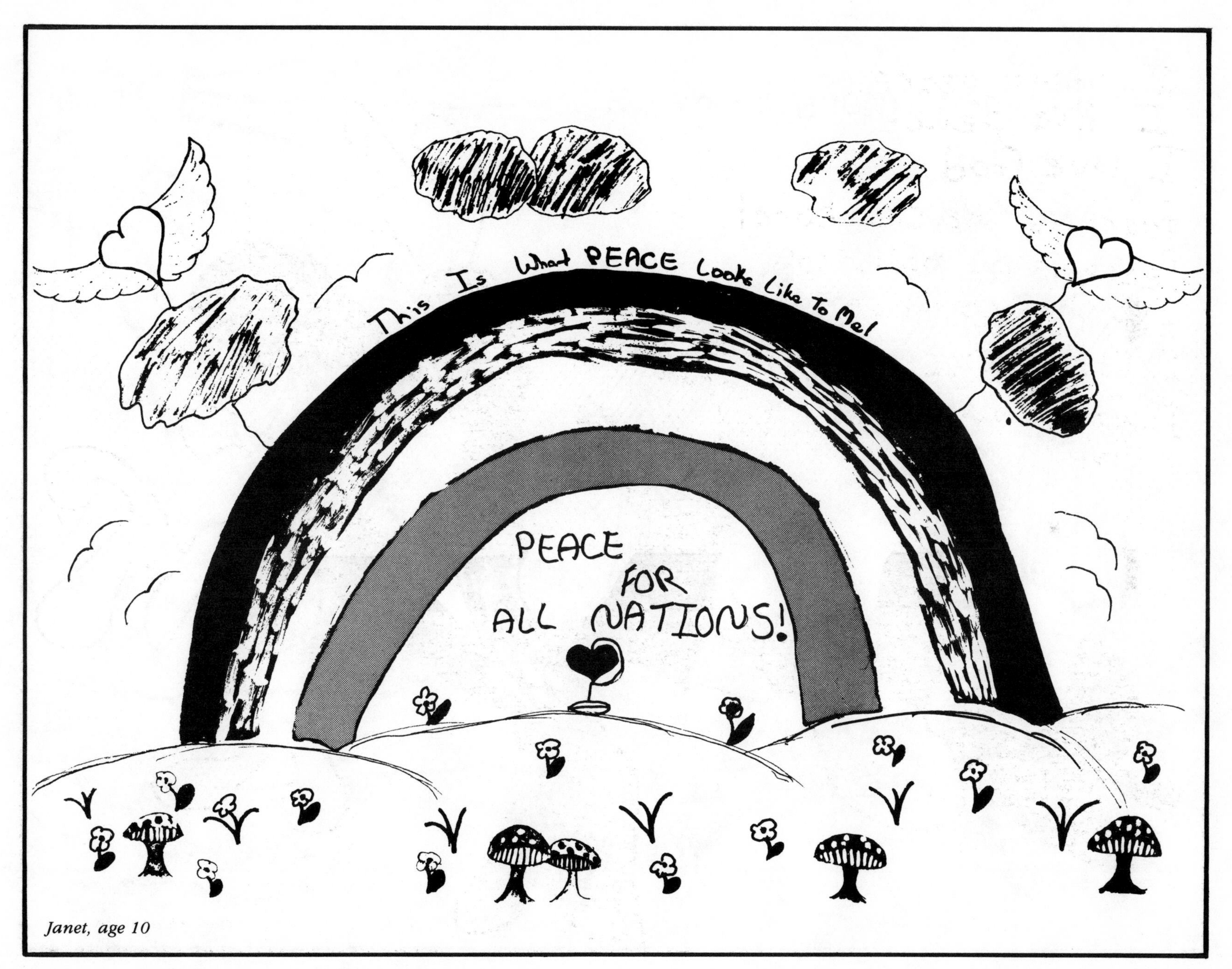

Janet, age 10

What peace means to me.....
Jessica a. K. age 11

Our Children Speak to Our Leaders

If I were a teacher to the world leaders, I'd say...

Dear Mr. Presadent,
I wrote befor to you butt
nothing seems to be happening
for one of the reasons I am
writeing to you is because I
really ment what I said
about not haveing Nuclear
war but when I watched
you on tv when I was
sick you just turned your
head when it cam to
That I hope this
time it works

Hannah Beth
Watson

JIM DAVIS

Dear Mr. Presadent,

I wrote befor to you butt nothing seems to be happening for one of the reasons I am writeing to you is because I really ment what I said about not having Nuclear war but when I watched you on tv when I was sick you just turned your head when it comes to That I hope this time it works.

Hannah Beth, age 10

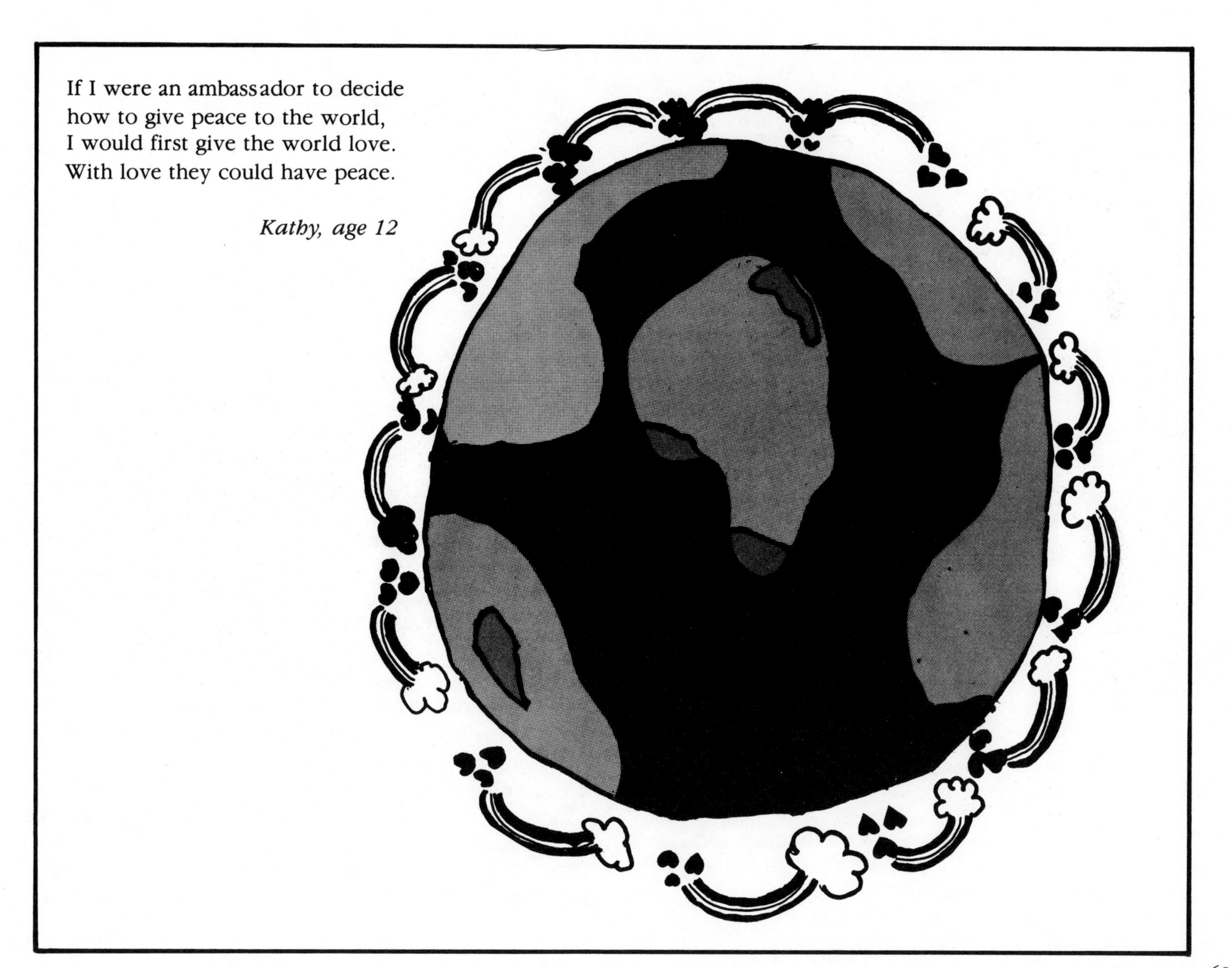

If I were an ambassador to decide
how to give peace to the world,
I would first give the world love.
With love they could have peace.

Kathy, age 12

If I were a teacher to the world leaders, I would tell them...

...when you and your country love your children more, there will be Peace forever. *Ernest, age 12*

... help bring peace to our world, don't be greedy, be nice to your enemies. And love one another.
Connie, age 11

...I only ask that people would try to understand what other people believe instead of automatically thinking, "I'm right, their wrong." Instead I wish they could say "I believe this; they believe in that. Maybe we could work out some kind of compromise." *Jeff, age 11*

...Tell all the big countrys to bug off the little countrys and all be friends. *Kasra, age 12*

Bahamas
United States
Denmark
Dominican Republic
Many ways to peace...
Jamaica
Argentina
Panama
Egypt
Cuba
Venezuela
Anna, age 13

If I were the teacher to
the world's leaders, I would
hold a conference with all
of them. I would teach them
that there should be no more
wars and no more hate
between nations. And I would
tell them to stop using
nuclear weapons. Lastly
I would tell them if any one
of them had a problem they
should come to me.

If I were the teacher to the world's leaders, I would hold a conference with all of them. I would teach them that there should be no more wars and no more hate between nations. And I would tell them to stop using nuclear weapons. Lastly I would tell them if any one of them had a problem they should come to me.

Rick, age 8

PEACE

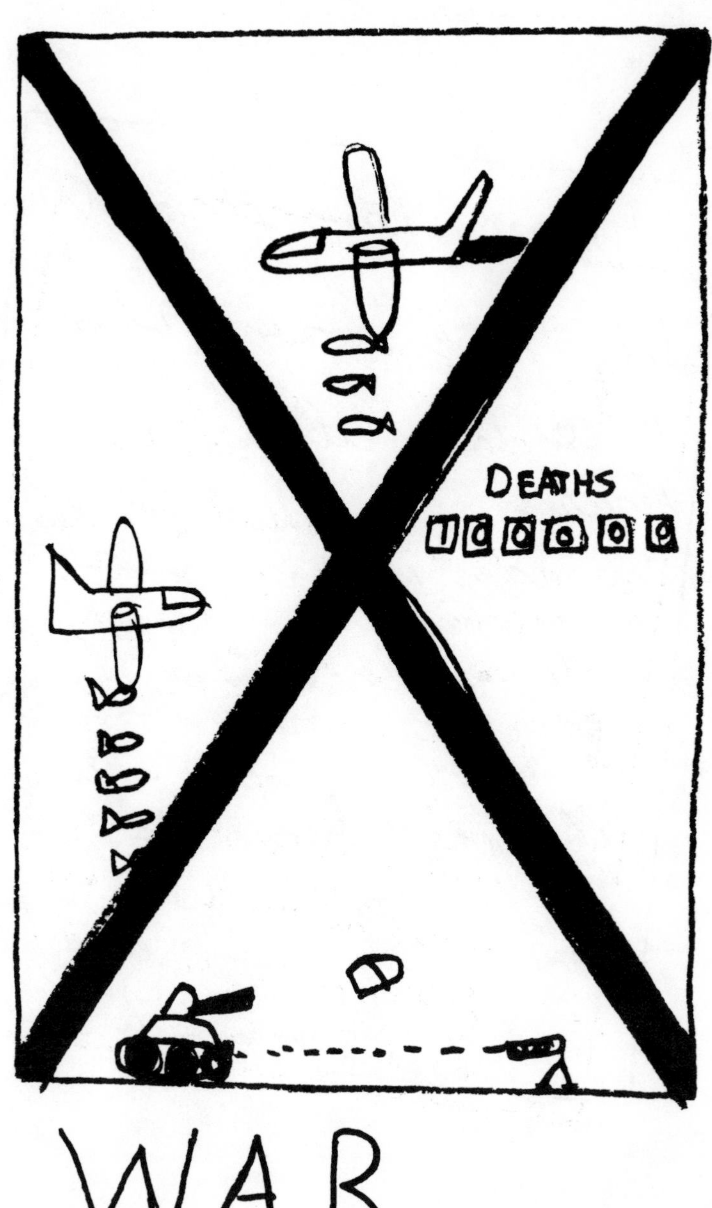

WAR

Wayne, age 11

Please have peace.

Why have wars? Nobody needs them. Alot of my realitives have died in them. too many innocent people have died in wars. And with nuclear and atomic bombs coming out, even more innocent people will die. why not sit down and talk like adults! Please have peace. Now if you press a button, a whole country is leveled out.

If I were a teacher to the world leaders, I would tell them. . . .

Please have peace. Why have wars? Nobody needs them. A lot of my relatives have died in them, too many innocent people have died in wars. And with nuclear and atomic bombs coming out, even more innocent people will die. Why not sit down and talk like adults! Please have peace. Now if you press a button, a whole country is leveled out.

Shaun, age 7

(Shaun's teacher: Shaun had tears in his eyes as he wrote this and left saying, "Mrs.__________, I got a lump in my throat while I was writing this. I wish things could be different than they are now but my feeling is it might never happen!")

Dear Mr. President,

I wish you would get together with Breshnev and other world leaders to figure out how we get rid of nuclear weapons. Nuclear weapons are a threat to my future. I am 10 years old and want to live to 100. How can I do this with the threat of nuclear war? The constitution says I have a right to live, but nuclear war threatens this right. In other words, nuclear war is unconstitutional. Please consider my future, and the future of all the children in the world.

Love,

Carrie, age 10

DEAR MR. PRESIDENT,

I WISH YOU WOULD GET TOGETHER WITH BRESHNEV AND OTHER WORLD LEADERS TO FIGURE OUT HOW WE GET RID OF NUCLEAR WEAPONS. NUCLEAR WEAPONS ARE A THREAT TO MY FUTURE. I AM 10 YEARS OLD AND WANT TO LIVE TO 100. HOW CAN I DO THIS WITH THE THREAT OF NUCLEAR WAR? THE CONSTITUTION SAYS I HAVE A RIGHT TO LIVE, BUT NUCLEAR WAR THREATENS THIS RIGHT. IN OTHER WORDS, NUCLEAR WARFARE IS UNCONSTITUTIONAL. PLEASE CONSIDER MY FUTURE, AND THE FUTURE OF ALL THE CHILDREN IN THE WORLD.

LOVE,

CARRIE KALINOWSKI

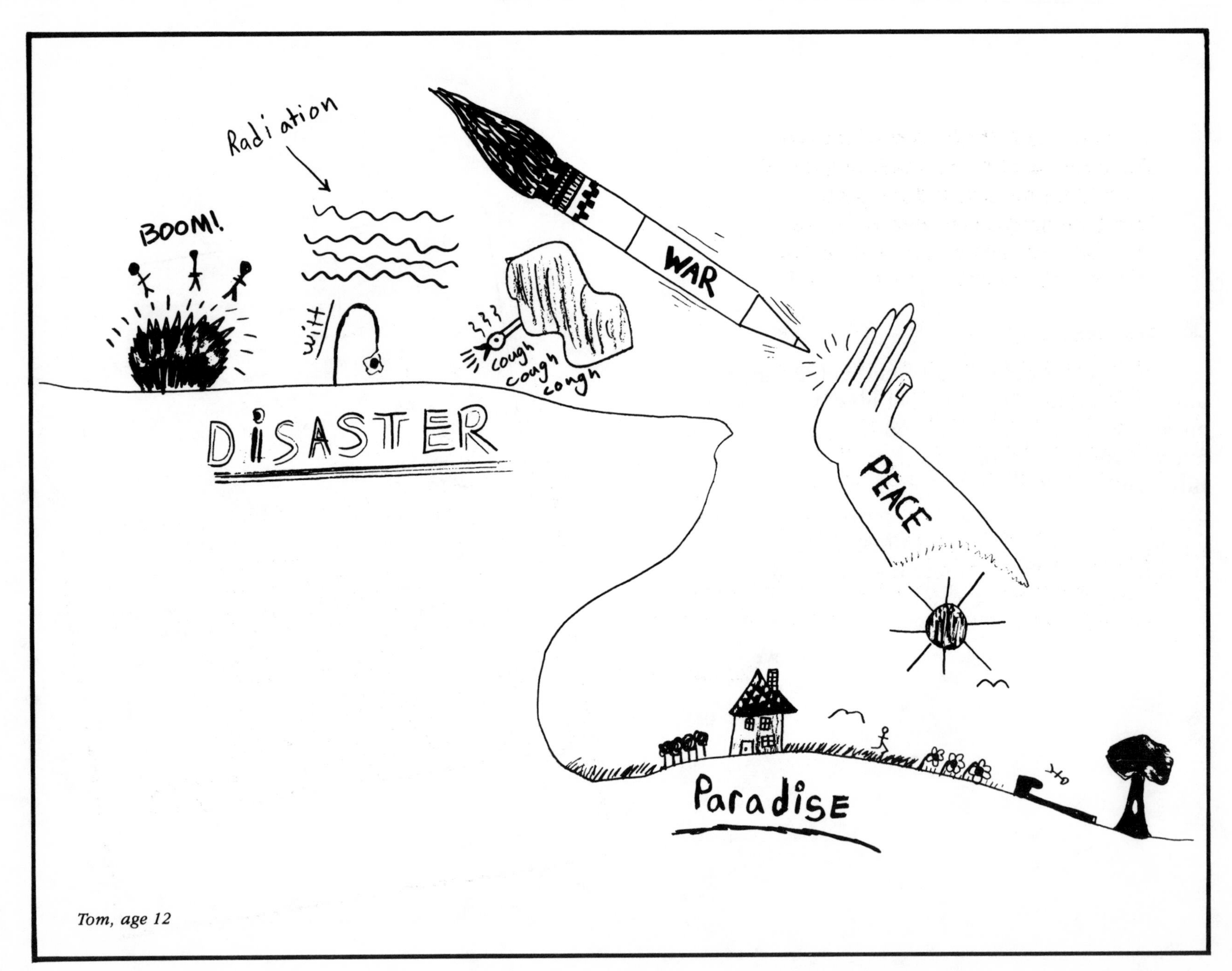
Radiation
BOOM!
with
cough
cough
cough
WAR
PEACE
DISASTER
Paradise

Tom, age 12

If I could teach the leaders of the world,
The meaning of peace and brotherhood.
I would say to each and everyone,
"Let your quarrels be over and done!"
"May all your nations join and be one!"
"Great and peaceful under the sun!"

Very soon I think they'd realize,
That their enemy is nothing to despise.
Of talk about nuclear arms and war,
Soon there would be no more.
As soon as silence had been found,
I'd tell them all to look around.

What they would see, would be a circle,
A circle of peace, a circle of people.
They would find that they had stumbled upon,
The fact that peace is togetherness, all nations one.

Bill, age 11

If I could teach the leaders of the world,
The meaning of peace and brotherhood.
I would say to each and everyone,
"Let your quarrels be over and done!"
"May all your nations join and be one!"
"Great and peaceful under the sun!"

Very soon I think they'd realize,
That their enemy is nothing to despise.
Of talk about nuclear arms and war,
Soon there would be no more.
As soon as silence had been found,
I'd tell them all to look around.

What they would see, would be a circle,
A circle of peace, a circle of people.
They would find that they had stumbled upon,
The fact that peace is togetherness, all nations one.

LEND A HAND! TO THIS LAND!
UNITEDNATIONS
IT'S THE WHOLE WORLD WE'RE DOING IT FOR! DAWN EllERMAN, 11

Ericia, age 11

If I were a teacher to the world leaders, I would say...

...to the leaders of a country, a few more casualties in a war is nothing. But to the families of these people, war has taken away a part of their hearts and lives. Leaders should realize that being imperialistic is not worth one family's suffering.

Jack, age 12

...never put any one else down. Because everyone makes mistakes. And I would also say always get along with other people. That's what I would say to bring peace in the world.

Gloria, age 10

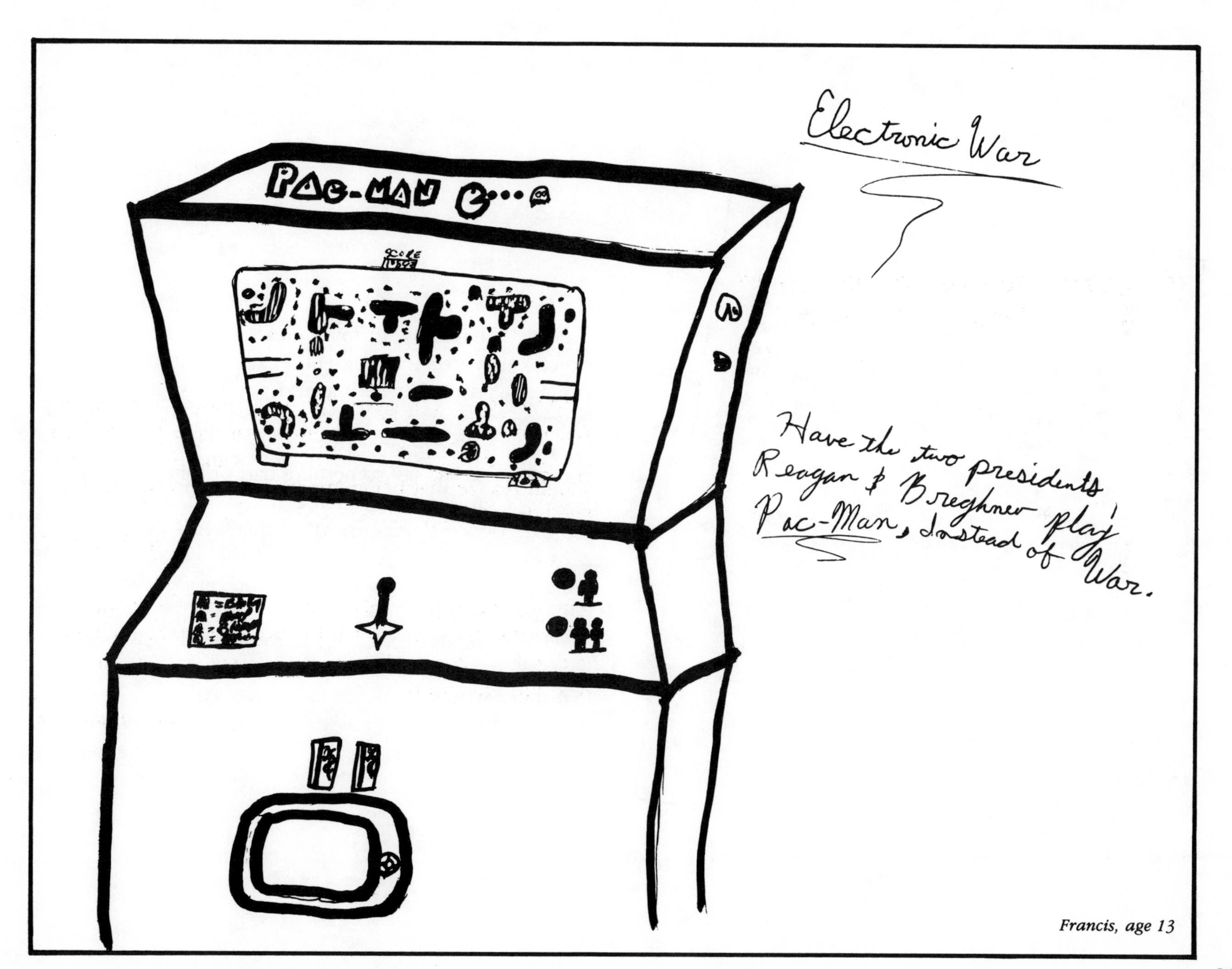

Francis, age 13

Carrie Kalinowski

Composition

Peace is having your mind clear of evil thoughts which can start an arguement. Peace is not holding a grudge against other people and not getting revenge. Revenge will never help. Why do people have to kill each other? The answer is they don't. When you know you are about to say something bad or when you are holding a grudge against someone, say to yourself, "I can experience peace instead of this." It is hard to do because a lot of people don't have the will to forgive other people. Having a war, or fight, or arguement is the easy way out.

If I were able to teach the world leaders, I would teach them to love, forgive, and experience peace. After that, there would be peace in the world.

. . .Peace is having your mind clear of evil thoughts which can start an arguement. Peace is not holding a grudge against other people and not getting revenge. Revenge will never help. Why do people have to kill each other? The answer is they don't. When you know you are about to say something bad or when you are holding a grudge against someone, say to yourself, "I can experience peace instead of this." It is hard to do because a lot of people don't have the will to forgive other people. Having a war, or fight, or arguement is the easy way out.

If I were able to teach the world leaders, I would teach them to love, forgive, and experience peace. After that there would be peace in the world.

Carrie, age 10

Dear Senator,

My brother, my parents, and a couple of thousand more are very scared and mad about the arms race.

My brother is 9 years old. Do you think that it is fair for him to die! If Russia drops a nuclear bomb on us the world will be destroyed along with thousands of people most of whom haven't lived their lives.

I have a wonderful friend who lives in Vermont. Her name is Erica Tepfer. She is 2½ years old. She moved there last July. I spend sleepless nights afraid of never seeing her before she comes back!

I would just like to know your opinion. Why do we have to be bigger than Russia? Why can't we leave each other alone?

I am ten years old and I live in Mendocino, California. You probably won't pay any attention to me but I would like you to know one thing. I want to live! I want to be able to grow up and have a family! I want to have a job and be happy! But all I have to look forward to is being killed by a nuclear bomb.

Caitlin, age 10

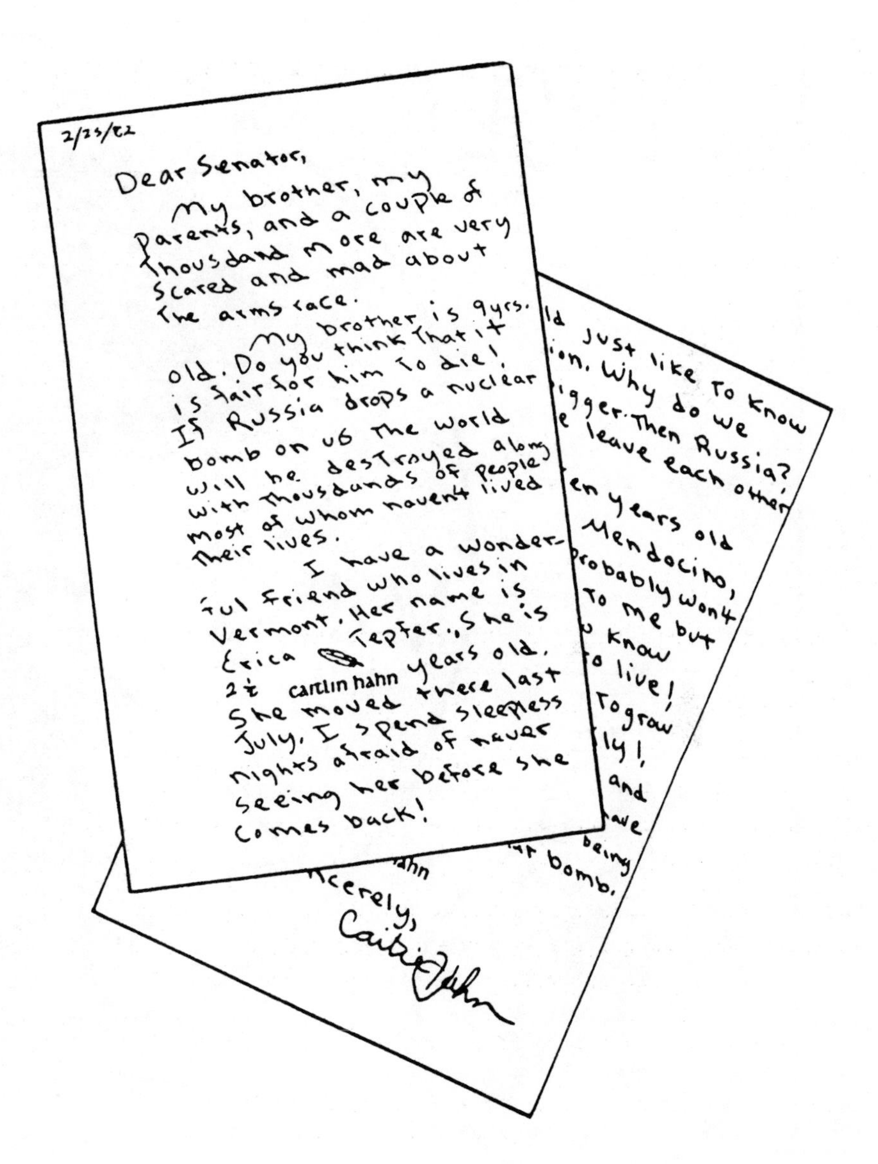

2/23/82

Dear Senator,

My brother, my parents, and a couple of thousand more are very scared and mad about the arms race.

My brother is 9yrs. old. Do you think that it is fair for him to die! If Russia drops a nuclear bomb on us the world will be destroyed along with thousands of people most of whom haven't lived their lives.

I have a wonderful friend who lives in Vermont. Her name is Erica Tepfer. She is 2½ years old. She moved there last July. I spend sleepless nights afraid of never seeing her before she comes back!

caitlin hahn

...ncerely,

Caitlin Hahn

PEACE!
Sarah
Louise
Wilkinson
age 9
NO!
NO!
HELP
YES!
YES!

Patricia, age 12

Dear Mr. President,

On the news every day, I hear of our problems with nuclear arms. I hear that people say we have enough arms to defeat Russia or any other country many times over.

People also say we need more weapons; we don't have enough; what if we get defeated? I think that we have enough arms to defeat any country. We are the leading power.

Instead of having to spend more money on weapons, we could get food for the starving, poor people in this world and do many other helpful things for people.

Sincerely yours,

Amynah Jammohamed age 10

Dear Mr. President,

On the news every day, I hear of our problems with nuclear arms. I hear that people say we have enough arms to defeat Russia or any other country many times over.

People also say we need more weapons; we don't have enough; what if we get defeated?

I think we have enough arms to defeat any country. We are the leading power.

Instead of having to spend more money on weapons, we could get food for the starving, poor people in this world and do many other helpful things for people.

Sincerely yours,

Amynah, age 10

ROB HARRIS, AGE 11

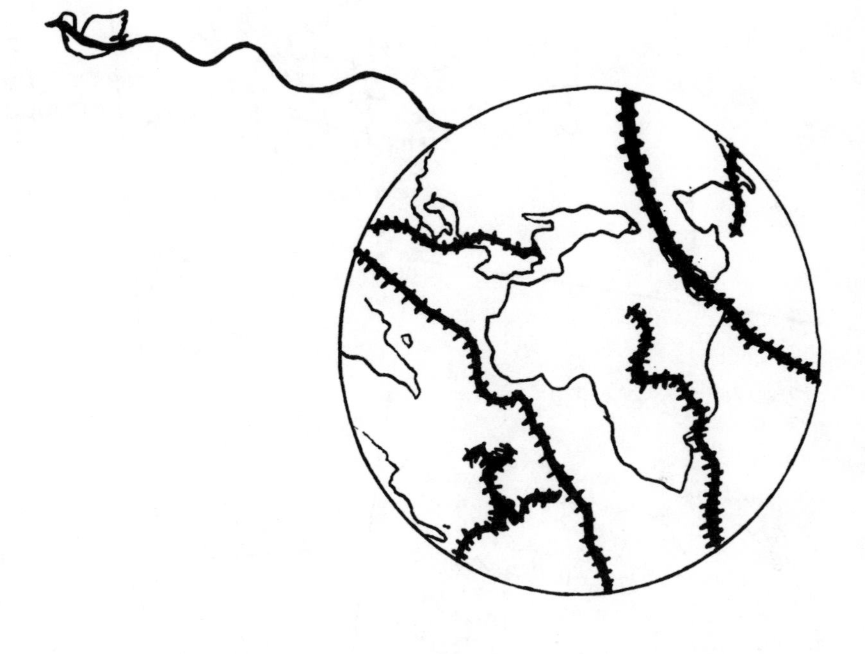

TORN BY THE
SAVAGE ACTS OF
WAR

MENDED BY
PEACE

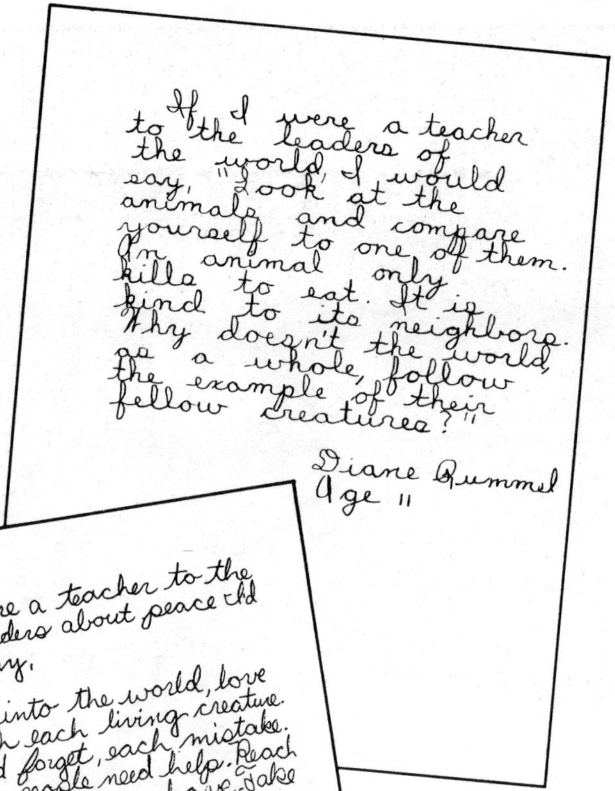

If I were a teacher to the leaders of the world, I would say, "Look at the animals and compare yourself to one of them. An animal only kills to eat. It is kind to its neighbors. Why doesn't the world, as a whole, follow the example of their fellow creatures?"

Diane Rummel
Age 11

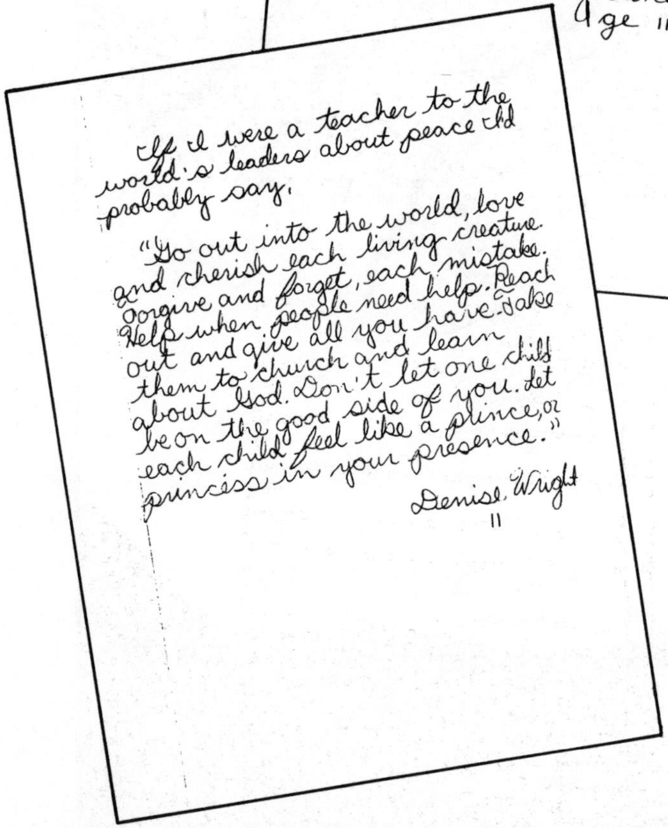

If I were a teacher to the world's leaders about peace I'd probably say,

"Go out into the world, love and cherish each living creature. Forgive and forget, each mistake. Help when people need help. Reach out and give all you have. Take them to church and learn about God. Don't let one child be on the good side of you. Let each child feel like a prince, or princess in your presence."

Denise Wright
11

If I were a teacher to the leaders of the world, I would say, "Look at the animals and compare yourself to one of them. An animal only kills to eat. It is kind to its neighbors. Why doesn't the world, as a whole, follow the example of their fellow creatures?"

Diane, age 11

If I were a teacher to the world's leaders about peace I'd probably say, "Go out into the world, love and cherish each living creature. Forgive and forget each mistake. Help when people need help. Reach out and give all you have. Take them to church and learn about God. Don't let one child be on the good side of you. Let each child feel like a prince or princess in your presence.

Denise, age 11

Peace and Brotherhood

Brad, age 7

If I were a teacher to the world leaders, I would say...

...Mr. President, I know you already know all this which could happen, will happen eventually, but please don't bring on our nation nuclear warfare. I'm in 5th grade going on to 6th grade and I want to see 7th, 8th, and 9th grade, without nuclear warfare. I would like to live a rich, full life like your own; to live as many years as *you* have enjoyed. Please allow me to enjoy the gift of life in our world. *Charley, age 11*

...War is for both sides but in the end we both lose. *Adam, age 12*

...Don't destroy what God created. *Ashley, age 11*

...If everyone would realize we are one world, I think PEACE would come about. *Leslie, age 11*

Lisa, age 10

If I were a teacher to the world's leaders, what I would say to them to help bring peace is....

Written by________________________ Age______

Drawn by ______________________ Age______

Now What?

If you want to learn more and do more about peace, here are a few suggestions:

Take time to listen: Listen to yourself, to children and to everyone.

Quiet your mind and listen to your heartfelt thoughts about the word "peace" and all it means to you. As you feel yourself becoming peaceful, extend this feeling of peace to everyone around you starting with your family, your friends and neighbors and all those in your immediate community. Now extend this same peace to everyone in this country and in all the countries of our world.

Share your thoughts on peace with your friends and ask your friends to share their thoughts on peace with others. Only by joining together can we bring peace to the world.

Look around you, in your family and community, school and church, for ways to assist children to express themselves about peace. This book is the result of a few hours commitment by a few people. Think what you can do. Do it! Let us hear about it.

To write to us or to be in touch with other people who are working for peace, please send a self-addressed, stamped envelope to "Children as Teachers of Peace," 98 Main Street, Suite 218, Tiburon, California 94920.

You can read other books about rediscovering the peace and love within yourself:

The Peace Book by Bernard Benson, published by Bantam books.

A Book of Games, There is a Place Where You are Not Alone, and *The Quiet Answer,* all by Hugh Prather, published by Doubleday & Company.

Love is Letting Go of Fear by Gerald G. Jampolsky, M.D., published by Celestial Arts and Bantam Books.

To Give is To Receive: Mini Course for Healing Relationships and Bringing About Peace of Mind by Gerald G. Jampolsky, M.D., published by Mini Course, P.O. Box 1012, Tiburon, California 94920.

Now you know our thoughts on peace and love. What are yours?

The Editors

Epilogue

The clarity of a child's point of view can yet lead the way to peace in a troubled world. Our best attempts at peace have failed because they have been based on trying to change people and events rather than on accepting and trusting ourselves and each other.

Young children experience their connection with all things and reflect to us our natural state of mind—love. They are a true mirror of who we are. In the process of becoming adults, we forget our oneness and learn to feel separate and afraid. As each of us joins with the children in this book and simply thinks about the word "peace," we can experience peace. Minds that want only peace must join for that is how peace is obtained.

Let us choose therefore to be witnesses to each other that peace begins with us; let us have only loving and peaceful thoughts in our hearts and minds. And then let us extend that peace to our family and to all those in the world so that the world can be transformed by a peace that is everlasting.

In love and peace,

Jerry

Gerald G. Jampolsky, M.D.

Credits

Name	*Hometown*	*Page*
Amana Ababio	Oakland, CA	58
Billy Adams	*	Title page
Leslie Alexander	Petaluma, CA	90
Darrell Anton	Tacoma, WA	20
Heather Ashcraft	Aurora, CO	30
Marc Avner	Englewood, CO	63
Jeremy Baldwin	*	13
Adam Behle	Tiburon, CA	26
Lauren Belton	Belvedere, CA	13
Suzanne Blanck	Denver, CO	12
Marilee Bostic	Tacoma, WA	44
Trace Bowen	Littleton, CO	53
Yolanda Brackens	Tacoma, WA	41
Jesse Bromberg	Tiburon, CA	53
Arthur Brown	Denver, CO	13
Shannon Bryant	Tiburon, CA	30
Brad Buchanan	Marietta, GA	89
Jeff Buckler	Louisville, KY	41
James Bunch	Tacoma, WA	41
Jessica Burton	Travis AFB, CA	13
Michael Celano	Durham, CT	30
Patricia Clark	Denver, CO	85
Jack Conway	Louisville, KY	80
Janet Coomes	Durham, CT	65
John Cowley	Tiburon, CA	41
Peter Crayne	Rohnert Park, CA	31
Penny Curran	Tacoma, WA	41
Bill Davis	Tiburon, CA	77
Sonny Davis	Travis AFB, CA	53
Lori Divita	Petaluma, CA	24, 25
Kasra Dowlatshahi	Tiburon, CA	70
Tappié Dufresne	Mill Valley, CA	14
Renee Dusoleil	Travis AFB, CA	53
Dawn Ellerman	Marietta, GA	78
Judith Eyre	Denver, CO	56
Ericia Fisher	Durham, CT	79
Terrance Fitzgerald	Englewood, CO	16
Mark Freeborn	Tacoma, WA	57
Marla Gaeddert	Denver, CO	45
Kendra Gaither	Ross, CA	30
John Garn	Santa Fe, NM	11
Cooper Glen	Belvedere, CA	53
Gloria*	Travis AFB, CA	80
Sari Goldstein	Aurora, CO	13
Wayne Guilmartin	Durham, CT	73
Sandy Gumz	Durham, CT	41
Caitlin Hahn	Mendocino, CA	83
Lashawn Haliburton	Denver, CO	13
Crista Hargreaves	Sedalia, CO	34
Kariena Harmon	Tacoma, WA	33
Rob Harris	*	87
Francis Hendrix	San Francisco, CA	81
Tom Herrin	Rohnert Park, CA	18
Nancy Heyns	Sedalia, CO	53
Brett Holsclaw	Louisville, KY	42
Gregory Howe	Denver, CO	Front cover
Amy Human	Denver, CO	53
Christine Hwang	Denver, CO	28
Jim Inman	Tacoma, WA	53
Amynah Janmohamed	Durham, CT	59, 86
Shae Jensma	Sedalia, CO	30
David Jolley	Mill Valley, CA	46
Christine Joy	Littleton, CO	35
Carrie Kalinowski	Durham, CT	75, 82
Clifford Kalinowski	Durham, CT	48
Ek Ong Kar Singh Khalsa	Española, NM	30
Gurumittar Har Singh Khalsa	Española, NM	63, 64
Siri Guru Dev Kaur Khalsa	Española, NM	30
Lisa Knapp	Durham, CT	91
Robert Korenic	Littleton, CO	47
Linda Kuhn	Marietta, GA	53
Alisa Larte	*	13

Name	Hometown	Page
Lance Lawson	Denver, CO	9, 38
Eric Lee	Littleton, CO	62
Chuck Lewis	Denver, CO	17
Dana Linker	Tiburon, CA	13
Susanna McCabe	Travis AFB, CA	13
Kathy McDonald	Castro Valley, CA	39, 69
Katy McLaughlin	Kentfield, CA	37
Elizabeth Marks	Belvedere, CA	53
Marnie*	*	53
John Marotta	Travis AFB, CA	41
Tom Mataya	Tiburon, CA	76
Matt*	*	40
Ernesto Mattler	Tacoma, WA	20
Michael Meaux	Englewood, CO	41
Megan*	*	53
Sherief Meleis	Greenbrae, CA	53
Wednesday Meshorer	Denver, CO	61
Larisa Mihelich	Tacoma, WA	41
Haley Mitchell	Kentfield, CA	22, 23
Brian Moore	Denver, CO	13
Siobhain Mosley	Denver, CO	30
Christine O'Keeffe	Rohnert Park, CA	52
Cassie O'Pry	Sedalia, CO	41
Ashley Payne	*	90
Terri Parmelee	Durham, CT	29
Joel Pearce	Tiburon, CA	51
Bethany Pierce	Orangevale, CA	41
Julianne Pletcher	Tacoma, WA	53
Joelle Polesky	Kentfield, CA	50
Michelle Primock	Englewood, CO	41
Nathan Rae	*	13
Jessica Reynolds	Mill Valley, CA	66
Shaun Rich	Tacoma, WA	74
Sandra Anne Robertson	Louviers, CO	60
Jennifer Robinson	Tiburon, CA	30
Carey Ryan	*	21
Diane Rummel	Littleton, CO	27, 88
Adam Saltzman	Tiburon, CA	90
Ernest Sams	Belvedere, CA	70
Connie Savage	Travis AFB, CA	70
Jeff Saxe	Corte Madera, CA	70
Heather Schmidt	Littleton, CO	41
Kerri Sherneski	Durham, CT	41
Jennifer Simpson	Littleton, CO	36
Sarah Snyder	Denver, CO	57
Allison Stollmeyer	Tiburon, CA	30
Stacy*	*	32
Shannon Stubo	*	67
Deanna Sturm	Travis AFB, CA	53
Allan Sugarbaker	Oakland, CA	13
Sirena Tabet	Corte Madera, CA	15
Carrie Taylor	Denver, CO	49
Anna Thomas	Austell, GA	71
Charlene Thomas	Spanaway, WA	33
Paxton Tucker	Louisville, KY	13
Rick Vangrin	Corte Madera, CA	72
Leigh Walton	Sedalia, CO	19
Hannah Beth Watson	San Anselmo, CA	68
Leigh Whelan	Louisville, KY	26
Melissa White	Durham, CT	41
Charley Wickham	Durham, CT	90
Sarah Louise Wilkinson	Mill Valley, CA	84
Justin Williams	Sedalia, CO	41
Michelle Willoughby	Littleton, CO	41
Natashya Wilson	Berkeley, CA	Back cover
Joan Worsley	Louisville, KY	30
Denise Wright	Littleton, CO	88

**Contribution did not include this information*